ERICA SPINDLER
Heaven Sent

Silhouette Desire

Published by Silhouette Books New York

America's Publisher of Contemporary Romance

For Nathan

SILHOUETTE BOOKS
300 East 42nd St., New York, N.Y. 10017

ISBN: 0-373-05442-4

First Silhouette Books printing August 1988

Printed in the U.S.A.

"Nice? Is That What You Look For In A Man?"

"Of course," Jessica snapped. "What should I look for? Hairy barbarians? Disreputable bums?"

Clay jerked his head toward her date, who'd stopped to talk to someone. "It'd beat the hell out of stodgy geezers in wing-tip shoes. Now I know why you don't mind if he's late—being alone is just as exciting as his company."

"How would you know what excites me?" she demanded.

"I know this—" Clay hauled her abruptly against his chest, his gaze capturing hers "—I could excite you. I could make it so that every minute I was late, you would tremble with anticipation of my touch."

"You think so, do you?" Her voice was suddenly, unrecognizably breathy.

"I know so."

"You're arrogant and conceited," she whispered, words her only remaining defense.

"Thank you," he murmured. "You'll never call me 'nice,' Jess."

Dear Reader:

Welcome! You hold in your hand a Silhouette Desire—your ticket to a whole new world of reading pleasure.

A Silhouette Desire is a sensuous, contemporary romance about passions, problems and the ultimate power of love. It is about today's woman—intelligent, successful, giving—but it is also the story of a romance between two people who are strong enough to follow their own individual paths, yet strong enough to compromise, as well.

These books are written by, for and about every woman that you are—wife, mother, sister, lover, daughter, career woman. A Silhouette Desire heroine must face the same challenges, achieve the same successes, in her story as you do in your own life.

The Silhouette reader is not afraid to enjoy herself. She knows when to take things seriously and when to indulge in a fantasy world. With six books a month, Silhouette Desire strives to meet her many moods, but each book is always a compelling love story.

Make a commitment to romance—go wild with Silhouette Desire!

Best,

Isabel Swift
Senior Editor & Editorial Coordinator

ERICA SPINDLER

came to writing from the visual arts and has numerous one-person, invitational and group exhibitions to her credit. She still teaches art classes in addition to her writing. "It seems only natural to me that I should be writing romance," says Erica. "My paintings had the same spirit of optimism and romanticism that my stories do."

A descendant of Marie Duplessis, who was the most famous courtesan of her day and the inspiration for Dumas's work *Camille*, Erica lives with her husband in New Orleans, where she does most of her writing in a penthouse that affords a panoramic view of that intriguing, history-rich city.

One

───

Hi, sweet thing. What's news?'' Clay Jones tossed the question and the package he was carrying at the receptionist. He grinned as she caught the package then turned it over in her hands.

"What's this?" she asked suspiciously.

"Fish," he answered, the grin coloring his tone.

"How thoughtful. I'm sure Charles and the kids will be ecstatic."

"Yeah, I aim to please." He laughed as she screwed up her face in distaste. "Now, Babs, that fish is rich in iodine and protein. You should be honored. I didn't bring any for anyone else."

"Not even the bosses?" Barbara made a clucking sound with her tongue.

"Uh-uh. Now, don't you feel special?"

"Oh sure, I'm underwhelmed."

Clay craned his neck in the direction of the executive offices. "Speaking of the boss, is he in? My flight was—"

"Bosses," Barbara interrupted. "Plural, as in two."

His eyebrows shot up at the laughter in her eyes. "Okay, Babs, spill it."

"Spill what?" she asked innocently.

"Don't play dumb with me. There's a definite gleam in your eyes, a gleam that spells a juicy piece of gossip you're delighted I don't already know. Now..." He lowered his voice to mimic Bogart and, placing his palms on the desk, leaned toward her. "Give up the goods, sweetheart."

"Since you've twisted my arm." Barbara smiled and looked furtively over her shoulder before continuing, "The Mann Agency has a new vice-president." She took a deep breath before delivering the pièce de résistance. "It's none other than Bill's elder daughter Jessica."

"No kidding." Clay cocked his head and scratched his beard. "That *is* news. Last I heard she was with a New York agency.... Ad House Inc., wasn't it?"

"Yup, she was. Bill hired her away from them. And guess what?"

Clay rolled his eyes. "There's more? You're just a mine of information."

"If you're going to keep repaying me with fish," she shot back, "remind me to keep my big mouth shut."

"Yeah?" He folded his arms across his chest. "Got any preferences?"

"Chocolates...very expensive chocolates." When he nodded, she continued. "You're going to be working with Jessica on the cookie account. And I warn you, she's a back buster." Barbara nudged his arm. "Speak of the devil, there she is...stepping off the elevator."

"Aha, the plot thickens." Clay swung around to get a look at the new VP. She was unnaturally still as she listened to something the copywriter was saying. Sunlight streamed over her, washing out the already fair skin and golden hair. She held herself in a way that shouted both breeding and control; her features bespoke ancestors who would have answered only to the king himself. She possessed a classic, even icy, beauty that reminded Clay of a Rodin sculpture in marble he'd once seen. Cheekbones slanted high in her face. Her nose was small and delicately chiseled, her eyes widely spaced and almond-shaped. Her pale skin looked as cool and smooth as the marble had, and her mouth seemed sculpted not for pleasure, but for purpose.

She exuded cool confidence and impeccable professionalism. A princess, he decided. An uptight, conservative and demanding princess. And she wouldn't like him. He was sure of that. He grinned over his shoulder at Barbara. "You'd better go and refrigerate your fish, and I'd better go meet mine."

Jessica stepped off the elevator, every epithet she'd ever heard racing through her head. She was furious. The man couldn't be trusted—he was unpredictable and totally unprofessional. For the creative director to miss the initial meeting with the client was unforgivable. When she saw him she would—

"Excuse me, Jessica. Do you have a moment?"

Jessica reined in her anger and flashed a small smile at the copywriter. "Certainly, Liz. What seems to be the problem?"

As Jessica listened, her gaze wandered over Liz's shoulder and focused on the man perched on the corner of the receptionist's desk. He looked like a barbarian, like a man who had little need of civilization and none for convention. Jessica's clear blue eyes narrowed as they flicked over him. Long and shaggy dark blond hair swept over his ears and collar, and his face was hidden by a beard that was heavy and untrimmed. It had no doubt been months since the man's cheeks had felt the edge of a razor. Both his army fatigue jacket and jeans were frayed; a backpack was slung carelessly over his shoulder and a motorcycle helmet dangled from his right hand.

So this is our hotshot, Jessica fumed, instinctively knowing that the man was Clay Jones. This...this cross between a beach bum and a hoodlum was the legend that her father had called "the best." She clenched her fingers around the handles of her portfolio at the thought.

"So, Jessica, which direction do you think would be the most effective?"

Jessica yanked her attention back to the copywriter. "They'd both effectively sell the product. Now it's a matter of esthetics. Let's see a layout with both headlines before we make the final decision."

"I'll have them on your desk by one."

"Fine," Jessica murmured, her gaze already returning to the barbarian. Their eyes met and tangled. His were dancing with humor and she suspected he was laughing at her. Her spine stiffened. This was a man who took from life without regrets and without worry about playing by the rules. And he was laughing at her because he sensed she lived only by the rules.

It irritated her and she glared at him. She didn't care what he thought of her. Not in the least. But why was the beastly man standing there staring at her as if he knew her deepest secret and was determined to use it against her? She drew her eyebrows together. Ridiculous—he was the one who'd better worry.

Jessica tossed her alligator portfolio onto the couch and strode across the room. Squaring her shoulders, she faced Clay Jones. "You're late," she said, folding her arms across her chest. "Do you realize that your tardiness could have cost us an important client? This morning's meeting was scheduled in order to begin formulating the creative direction for the Cookies from Heaven campaign. It would have been nice if the creative director had bothered to show up."

His eyes narrowed slightly for a moment before he smiled. The curving of his lips was slow and wicked. "Well, hello to you, too. I'm Clay."

"I know who you are," Jessica snapped, furrowing her eyebrows again.

"You shouldn't do that too often," he drawled, resting his hips against the desk and folding his arms in imitation of her gesture.

"Excuse me?"

Clay tapped the space above his nose and between his eyes with his index finger. "Draw your eyebrows together. Wrinkles."

"Oh?" *He's not only unkempt,* Jessica decided, *but insane as well.* Outrage curled through her. "Do you know who you're talking to?"

The corner of his mouth lifted as her eyes filled with heat. "Yeah, Jessica Mann, Daddy's darling and new vice-president. Babs filled me in." He touched an imaginary brim. "Glad to meet you, Jess."

"Jessica," she corrected.

"Whatever." Cocking his head, he shoved his hands into his pockets. "So…Jess, why don't you grab your 'gator so we can take off?"

Jessica took a deep breath and counted to ten. After only five minutes the man was driving her crazy. A half-hour from now she would be ready for a straitjacket. By the time they finished the campaign she would be a vegetable. "Grab my what and let's go where?"

He tucked her arm through his. "Portfolio and to lunch."

Her father had said that Clay was eccentric. Eccentric? The man was a lunatic, a card-carrying maniac. He talked in circles and dodged responsibility like a child dodged spinach. "Lunch?" Jessica's tone was incredulous. "It's only ten-forty."

"But in Wisconsin it's going on one o'clock, and my stomach's still on central time."

"That may be, but I have no intention of stopping for lunch right now. My calendar is full today."

"Your loss and precisely my point." Clay shrugged and turned toward the elevator.

"What do you mean by that?" Jessica asked, despite her resolve not to.

Clay stopped, turning back to her. "Well, we need to get together sometime and we're both free now. It seems like a perfect opportunity for you to fill me in on this morning's meeting and discuss your feelings about the direction we should take."

He was right. Her afternoon was booked solid. It really made no difference if they talked here or in the coffee shop. Jessica nodded curtly and followed him out of the office and into the elevator. Her father might think this man was the best, but he looked like a barbarian, acted like a mental-institution escapee and probably had the eating habits of both. And she was going to have lunch with him. A frustrated sigh escaped her.

"I heard that." Clay shot her an amused look.

"Excuse me?"

"You sighed."

"You're mistaken."

"Mmm, you did. It was an annoyed sigh." He took her elbow and steered her toward the restaurant. "Let's be honest with one another. You want to get down to business. For you there's nothing else. You think my behavior and appearance are bizarre and you're only tolerating me—probably because your father insisted I work on this account." He slipped into the booth and took a seat opposite her. "How'd I do?"

Irritation would be an understatement, anger an afternoon in the park—she was livid. The hotshot was right again. He was her father's choice and there was nothing she could do about it. Jessica met his eyes squarely. "You did very well, Mr. Jones."

"Clay."

"Whatever." A hint of a smile curved her lips at having returned that one before she continued. "If we're being honest, your behavior and appearance are bizarre. In fact, you look like the type of man who would dine at a place called EATS, and I suspect your manners would match your choice of restaurant. You have no desire to discuss business or to spend more time with me than absolutely necessary. Am I correct?"

"Jessica," he drawled, smiling and resting his chin on his fist, "you wound me. There's no place I'd rather be."

She released her breath in a sudden huff. The man was impossible. Folding her arms across her chest once more, she stuck out her chin and glared at him as he ordered lunch.

"Would you like anything besides coffee?" Clay asked, handing the waitress the menu.

"No, thank you. Shall we get down to business?" Jessica pulled out her notes. "How much do you already know about the account?"

"I've done my homework...Jess." When her spine stiffened, a grin twitched at the corners of his lips. "Cookies from Heaven is a family-owned-and-operated business. It started out as a mom-and-pop organization with one store in Laguna Beach. In this case the 'mom and pop' are brother and sister. They now have thirty-four stores throughout California and are planning to advertise for the first time."

"Very good." Jessica paused to sip the black coffee the waitress had set in front of her. "A few months ago Ty and Sandra Miller approached us about bidding for their advertising. We were one agency out of ten."

"Your former agency was one of the group." It wasn't a question; he'd read about the finalists for the Cookies from Heaven account in *Adweek*.

A smile flickered across her face. "Yes."

"Victory is sweet."

"Mmm." The smile continued to tug at her mouth, so Jessica gave in and laughed. "Sweeter than strawberries at the peak of season, more satisfying than a box of chocolates on a rainy afternoon." She drew her eyebrows together as she lowered her eyes to her notes. "This morning Ty and Sandra confirmed what I'd only suspected. Their decision to advertise is the first stage in their move to expand the business. Ultimately they want their product marketed nationwide."

Clay stared at her in surprised silence. Where had those flowery words come from? Whimsy from a woman like Jessica Mann was enough of an anomaly, but perfect whimsy?

"Their decision couldn't have come at a better time, both for us and for Cookies from Heaven. The market's ripe for this type of product; the exotic, the unusual, the expensive are in." She paused as the waitress delivered his order, then continued. "Searching for the better-tasting, so-called gourmet anything has become a national trend. Our marketing department has done a study of related food items." Jessica handed him the report. "Look at the way the sales of the more expensive, gourmet ice creams have climbed in the last two years."

"Frozen foods and candies are showing the same growth. Pass the catsup, will you?"

Jessica handed him the bottle. "This type of impetus is pure gold."

"Fourteen karat," Clay murmured before taking a large bite of his cheeseburger.

Jessica eyed his choice of lunch. Greasy cheeseburger and fries, plus a sugar-laden soft drink. "You obviously don't subscribe to the gourmet trend."

"Nope." Clay dipped a French fry into catsup. "Let them all eat Black Forest cake. I'm perfectly satisfied with junk food."

"That's fine with me as long as your arteries don't clog before we finish the campaign."

His eyes swept slowly over her. "You must have a weakness . . . Jess. Surely you're not in control of everything in your life?"

Jessica stiffened. She wouldn't let him rile her, she simply would not. "My life is no concern of yours," she returned coolly, checking her watch. "I have another appointment in ten minutes. Let's wrap this up."

Grinning at the way her eyes had heated, Clay wiped his mouth with the paper napkin, then pushed his plate aside. "Okay, what are we shooting for?"

"New logo, company stationery, package design for the cookies. They want primarily television, supplemented by print." Jessica gathered her things together and slid out of the booth. "I have some ideas for a direction, but I'd like to see your initial concept before we discuss mine." She checked her watch again. "Let's get together first thing in the morning. Nine?"

"Fine."

"Good, I'll see you then." With a brief nod she spun on her heels and walked away.

By eight o'clock that night Jessica was exhausted. Usually she came home exhilarated, no matter what time it was. But tonight her head throbbed, her shoulders ached. Blast Clay Jones! The man was a menace, a professional disaster. He'd started her day off in the pits and it had stayed there. Sighing, she unlocked the door of her condominium and stepped inside.

"Hi, Sissy. How was your day?" Alicia Mann was curled up on the taupe leather couch. She looked up from the magazine she was reading and smiled at her sister.

"Don't ask," Jessica muttered, tossing her portfolio onto the sofa and kicking off her pumps.

"That bad, huh?"

"Worse." Placing her fists on her hips she faced her sister. "Remember me telling you Dad had assigned the creative director for the cookie account—my account—despite my objections?"

"How could I forget?" Alicia asked dryly. "I've never seen you so hot." Her eyes skimmed over her sister. "Except for now."

"And I guarantee it's going to get hotter." Jessica rubbed her temples. "The creative director's name is Clay Jones. He's certifiably insane, dresses like a hoodlum and possesses as much professional decorum as the apes at the zoo."

Alicia laughed and set aside her magazine. "I met him once and thought he was cute. How about a glass of wine?"

"Cute? Cute!" Jessica blew at the wisps of hair that had somehow escaped her tidy coil and fallen into her eyes. She was sure that was also Clay Jones's fault. "You thought that huge, hairy ape was cute?"

"No accounting for taste, I guess. Although I don't remember him being hairy." Alicia stood, stretched and headed for the kitchen. "White or red?" she called from the doorway.

Jessica caught herself about to say "whatever" and gritted her teeth. "White, please." Removing her jacket, she tossed it on top of the portfolio, then sank onto the couch. The sigh she emitted was one of pure relief.

"You work too hard, Sis."

"Not true, Ali." She took a sip of wine, holding it for a moment on her tongue before swallowing. It was crisp and refreshing. "It's just that compared to you, I'm a workaholic."

"No, you *are* a workaholic." When Jessica made a face, Ali groaned. "Don't even try to deny it! It's eight o'clock at night and you're just walking in the door. You left at six-thirty this morning, and I'll bet you didn't stop for lunch."

Jessica frowned at her sister. "You're not being fair. Today wasn't an ordinary day; I had an early appointment with a new client. And you're wrong....I *did* stop for lunch." She didn't add that all she'd had was coffee; her sister didn't need any more ammunition. "Speaking of food, have you eaten?"

"Yes, but I made enough for two and am reheating yours at this very moment. It should be ready now."

"I love being pampered," Jessica murmured, following Alicia into the kitchen.

"You need to be pampered." Alicia shot her sister another disapproving look before opening the oven.

"You're never going to change me, Ali. Although I do appreciate all the time and effort you put into it." Jessica inhaled and sighed. "That's eggplant casserole, isn't it?"

"Uh-huh. And there are homemade wheat rolls and a tossed salad in the fridge."

Jessica thought of Clay Jones's greasy hamburger as she carried her plate to the table. Had it not been for her sister, her stomach would have suffered a similar fate this evening. "Ali, if you weren't my sister I'd ask you to marry me."

"Oh sure, you say that now, but what would you say if I asked to borrow your mauve silk dress?"

"Not the mauve silk?" Jessica made an outraged face, then took a bite of casserole. "Ohh, wonderful. Food for a queen. Take the mauve silk, Ali. Take the mauve accessories, the pearls...."

"You got it." Ali grinned and sipped her wine. "So tell me more about Clay Jones."

"He's impossible." Jessica waved her fork. "Unprofessional, unkempt, kooky. I can't believe father keeps hiring him back."

"Maybe you're exaggerating," Alicia suggested, her grin widening.

"Exaggerating? Me?" Jessica pointed at herself, then scowled. "He missed this morning's meeting with the client. If that's not unprofessional I don't know what is. Do you know where he's been?" Jessica didn't wait for a response. "Fishing! For four months!" She shuddered. "God, can you imagine fishing for four months?"

"He does good work."

"So do a lot of other artists—dependable, steady artists." Jessica viciously stabbed a bit of eggplant.

"You must have liked him."

"Ali, I can't believe you said that." Jessica glowered at her only sister. "Why did you say that?"

Alicia smiled sweetly and shrugged.

"Spill it, Ali. I'm in no mood for games."

"It's not often you *are* in the mood for games, but I love you, anyway." Alicia laughed as Jessica tilted her chin defensively. "Okay, okay... because your eyes are sparkling and your skin is glowing."

"Of course it is! I'm furious!"

"I rest my case."

Jessica took a deep, calming breath and glared at her sister. "Ali, you're as insane as he is. You should be locked up together; the key should be melted down or thrown into the ocean."

A smile twitched at the corners of Alicia's mouth. "I wouldn't kick him out of bed."

Jessica's eyes widened. "Ali, you're in desperate need of professional help."

"But don't worry," Alicia continued cheerfully. "I won't horn in on your territory."

Jessica narrowed her eyes at the comment. "I'd see you married to the hairy beast, with ten children, before I'd let him near me."

Alicia clucked her tongue. "You should never say never, Jessica."

The next morning Jessica stood at her office door, her hands wrapped around a coffee mug. She loved mornings, loved being the first to arrive at the agency. It was so quiet, so still. She found quiet in a place that usually shouted with activity somehow soothing.

Leaning her shoulders against the doorjamb, Jessica sipped the coffee and gazed at her office. It was a large, light room; she'd chosen it for both those reasons. This morning the sun spilled riotously through the windows, creating bright, magical shapes on the carpeting and walls.

She'd enjoyed every moment of planning the interior, from looking at paint and carpet samples to finding an original Art Deco poster for the wall behind her desk.

Jessica ran a finger along the leather and chrome Bauhaus chairs, rubbed away a water spot on her glass-topped desk, talked softly to the huge yucca tree in the corner. She'd worked hard for this office. She'd given up dates, and lived without vacations. Her twenties had flown by in a flurry of meetings and late-night paperwork and she was sure her thirties would bring more of the same. It had been, and still was, worth it. She'd proven to herself and her father that she could make it in the advertising business—his business.

Jessica stared out the window at downtown Los Angeles. It was the same view she enjoyed every day, the steel and glass high-rise buildings, the billboard announcing Universal Studio's newest release, the scattered palm trees. Her expression hardened as she thought of Clay Jones. She'd given up everything to prove to her father that she was a professional, that she could handle the pressure and make snap decisions. Clay Jones hadn't given up a thing and her father called him the best.

"What was it this time, Bill?" Jessica had demanded the week before. "Sunning in Mexico? Backpacking through Europe? Mountain climbing?"

Bill Mann tightened his mouth to a thin line. "He was fishing in Wisconsin."

"Surely not the whole time?" At her father's nod her eyes widened in disbelief, then narrowed with distaste. "This just reinforces my opinion of the man. I don't want him assigned to the cookie account. I need someone I can work with, someone I can depend on."

"You can depend on Clay," Bill said mildly. "He's a hard worker."

"*When* he's working," Jessica inserted caustically.

"True. But he never takes off until a job's complete. Trust me, Jessica. Clay's the right man for the job."

"I disagree." Jessica lifted her chin. "Look at his record—he's unpredictable, unprofessional."

"He's a little eccentric, that's all. Most artists are."

Sinking onto one of the two chairs facing her father's desk, she looked at him over steepled fingers. Since returning to the agency she'd heard story after story about the legendary Clay Jones. Stories ranging from elaborate practical jokes to award-winning designs to an after-hours beach party in the office. She'd been less than impressed.

"This is a business. If he wants to be eccentric, let him paint landscapes or nudes. You've given me complete control of the Cookies from Heaven account, and I'd like your okay to choose another creative director."

"No. The clients were impressed with his work on the Sally's Candies and Lite and Lovely accounts. You know that, Jessica."

She met his eyes in challenge. "I also know I could have changed their minds."

A slight flush crept over Bill's cheeks. "You may be in charge of this account, Jessica, but this is my agency. I want Clay as creative director. Is that clear?"

"Crystal clear, Bill." She curled her fingers into her palms, then shoved her hands into her blazer pockets. "Just tell me why. He keeps taking off whenever the whim strikes, and you keep taking him back. Why?"

A hint of a smile curved the corners of her father's mouth as he answered. "Because he's the best, Jessica. Because he's the best."

Jessica shook her head and turned away from the window. The fact that her father had shrugged off her opinion and pulled rank had both angered and hurt her. She'd worked damn hard to get where she was today, and he still didn't take her seriously. And it wasn't because she'd been a flighty child or a wild teenager—she hadn't been—it was because she was a daughter instead of a son. Sexism in the business world was rampant, but she'd learned long ago both to expect it and how to deal with it. Except when it came from her own father.

It had hurt the first time and it still did. At twelve she'd heard him lament over not having a son to take over his business someday. At seventeen she'd told him she wanted to go into advertising and had asked him for a part-time job. He'd smiled at the first and refused the second. He'd told her she didn't have to work, and suggested she study something practical when she went to college. Something like home economics or nursing. When she'd lifted her chin and dug in her heels, he'd told her she would have to prove to him that she could handle the pressure.

What he'd meant, she thought cynically, was prove that a *woman* could handle the pressure. Sighing, she turned toward her desk. Nothing had changed. He still didn't take her seriously; he'd never once complimented her. As the beginnings of a headache throbbed behind her eyes, she realized the magic had gone out of her morning.

Clay yawned, stretched and stared at the ceiling. He loved mornings. There was a magical quality to the light: softly brilliant and warming, yet without the harshness of midday. The air was sweet, as if cleansed of human pollutants by the black velvet of night. Nature's sounds were hushed whispers, whispers careful of waking those who still slumbered, sounds that coaxed the world back to life as one lover coaxes another.

Swinging his legs over the side of the bed, Clay walked nude onto the deck. His was a quiet stretch of beach, the deck protected from view on all sides but the one directly facing him. And what faced him was the ocean, sparkling like a billion diamonds in the sun, alive and wild and free. Its song was repetitive, yet filled with such subtle variations as to never be boring. And power—it hummed with a power to make the achievements of man seem small and facile.

He was home. As much as he loved traveling, as much as he enjoyed experiencing other landscapes, this little stretch of beach was home. He'd bought the house five years ago when he was still making six figures and had thanked God ever since for that decision.

Clay inhaled deeply. He could grow fat on the sweetness of this day, he thought. It was sweeter than strawberries at the peak of season, more satisfying than a box of chocolates on a rainy afternoon. His grin was crooked as he acknowledged both quoting Jessica and the way her image had flooded his mind as he did so. How could such a hard woman say something so soft? he wondered, absently scratching his chest. Maybe she was just hard on the outside, like a Tootsie Pop or a turtle. In the case of the first, the shell was covering a delicious treat. One had to work through the concealing layer to attain the special prize; it could be frustrating work but was always worth it. In the case of the turtle, the shell was a shield, a device to protect the softness and vulnerability of the occupant. Clay tipped his head to one side in thought; both theories were intriguing, both promised rich rewards.

Clay laughed, suddenly and with delight. He was a crazy romantic. Jessica Mann was just what she appeared to be: a hard-core business person. He'd met them in both sexes and all races. They were all the same. People scurrying up the ladder had no time for softness, no time for poetry. He should know; he'd been one of them for eight years. For eight years he'd been a man possessed by ambition, owned by the time clock. Never again. Laughing at his freedom, Clay turned his back on the ocean and went inside to dress.

Two

Jessica rubbed her temples and cursed having left her reading glasses at home. The contract blurred, her head throbbed, and she lifted her eyes. As she did so her gaze trailed from once-white running shoes over faded and patched jeans to a Mickey Mouse T-shirt stretched across a broad chest. He was standing in the doorway watching her. His stance was relaxed and confident and his eyes danced with amusement. Annoyance rippled through her.

"Morning, Jess."

"Good morning, Clayton."

"Clay," he corrected.

She smiled sweetly. "Jessica."

"Touché." He flashed her his most disarming grin as he crossed the room. "For you, Madam Vice-President."

Jessica arched an eyebrow, taking the small white bag from his hands. "What's this?"

"Look inside and find out." Clay lowered himself to the chair across from her. "Wanna wager a guess first?"

"You're leaving yourself open, Jones." Jessica opened the bag. "Pastries?"

"Yeah, cheese-filled croissants. Hope you like them."

"I love them. Will you join me?"

"Nope, they're both for you." He glanced around the room as he spoke. "Nice office. It fits you—all cool, clean lines."

"Why," she asked dryly, "do I suspect that's an insult?"

His eyes returned to hers. They were brilliant with laughter. "Dig in, Jess. You're too thin, you know."

For a moment—only a moment—she'd been touched by the simple gesture of the pastries. She'd misinterpreted them as a peace offering, as an acknowledgment that although they were two very different people they could forget their differences and work together for the good of the agency and the client. She'd been mistaken. He'd used them to needle her. Her cool blue eyes became glacial, then narrowed. "You are the most annoying man I've ever met."

He grinned at the insult. "Aw shucks, princess, not little old me?"

Princess? Princess! Determined to remain in control, she took a deep, steadying breath. "I'm afraid so. After all, everybody has to be the best at something." When Clay only laughed, Jessica frowned. The man couldn't even take an insult properly. She sat up straight in her chair and stared at him. She could deal with open hostility or veiled barbs, but this perpetual amusement was foreign to her. How did one calmly and rationally deal with insanity?

He cocked his head and scratched his beard. "Hmm... The most annoying man on earth. I would have preferred the sexiest or wittiest, but—"

"Stow it," Jessica interrupted with a grin she couldn't help, and handed him a napkin and a croissant. "I won't eat them both," she said as he opened his mouth to protest.

He shrugged, then took a large bite and murmured his approval. Jessica watched him finish the croissant in three bites, then lick his fingers. "Do you do everything with such gusto?"

"Everything," he answered, wiggling his eyebrows in an imitation of Groucho Marx.

Jessica groaned. A sexual innuendo from Clay Jones was laughable. He was the last person she would find attractive. He was huge and hairy, dressed like a slob, had the work ethic of a beach bum, and was as refined as grain alcohol. He could innuendo himself silly, but he would never pique her curiosity. A laugh caught in her throat at the absurdity of the thought. Clay Jones was no more interested in her than she in him. And that was fine with her. Just fine.

Looking up again, she smiled. "So, Clay, what do you have for me this morning?"

Clay blinked quickly in surprise. Her smile had been brief but warm, transforming her face the way sunlight transformed the landscape. Her features had suddenly seemed softer, her skin warmer, more pliant. He wondered why she smiled so rarely and wished she would smile again.

"Well?" Jessica raised one eyebrow. Why was he looking at her as if he'd figured her out? It made her uncomfortable, and she squirmed in her seat. "Is something wrong, Clay?"

The smile that curved his lips was slow and easy. "No, not a thing." He picked up his backpack and pulled out the roughs he'd carefully rolled and tucked inside, then spread them out on her desk. "Have the clients given you any indications of a direction?"

"No, they've put the creative totally in our hands." Lowering her eyes to the designs, she cleared her throat. "So what are your ideas?"

Clay followed her lead, becoming all business. "I've given this campaign a lot of thought. There are many directions we could take, but I think we should stick to a traditional one."

"You're kidding!" Jessica leaned forward to study his designs.

His eyes met hers. "Would I kid you, Jess?"

She pulled her gaze from his to scan the roughs. "By heaven, you're not!" She met his eyes again. "Why, Clay? We have a lot of creative leeway here; why not use it?"

"Simple. What do most people associate with yummy, wonderful cookies?"

"Home, hearth and Mom." Jessica made a small, annoyed gesture with her fingers. "But still—"

"No buts. Playing on those associations and conjuring up warm childhood memories will most effectively sell the product."

Jessica made a frustrated sound. "Effective—there's no question of that, it's a tried and true direction. But it's not necessarily the *most* effective. Why rely on a stereotyped approach to the product?" She tapped the rough for emphasis. "It's our job as designers and marketing experts to create new, better ways of selling an old product."

Clay absently toyed with the crumpled napkin on the desk in front of him. "What do you suggest?"

"I'd like to try a new wave approach." Jessica stood and began to pace. "I think we should go for high-tech slick. Totally unexpected and unprecedented for cookies." She swung around to face him. "Think of contemporary interior design, all funky shapes and neon, think of television graphics, like what's being done for MTV." Shoving her hands into the pockets of her thigh-length jacket, she faced him. "So?"

Clay expelled a long, thoughtful breath before beginning. "It sounds like an award winner. But a lot of award-winning campaigns don't sell the product." He began folding the napkin. "What's most important here, winning an award or selling the product?"

Her hands curled into balls in her pockets and she didn't try to relax them. "That's unfair and you know it." She tipped up her chin and glared at him. "First of all, we can have both. That's advertising at its best. Secondly, I believe my direction will work. Look at all the attention being paid to the upwardly mobile in this country. This last year you couldn't pick up a newspaper, magazine or journal without seeing an article about yuppies. That whole attitude is responsible for the surge in gourmet sales we discussed yesterday."

"Oh, come on, Jess." Clay set the carefully folded napkin aside. "By the looks of Cookies from Heaven's yearly sales figures, they're already getting those yuppie dollars, plus some. We have to persuade the people who can't afford to spend a dollar and a quarter on one cookie to do so. I say play on the emotions and memories of the buying public. Everybody's a sucker for that."

"We want to suck people in, Clay, not to sucker them."

"Semantics." He began toying with the other napkin.

Jessica tried another tack. "Look around you." She gave in to the need to gesture and pulled her hands out of her pockets. "We're basically a decadent society. We love flash and trash. We're conspicuous consumers. For the opening and closing ceremonies of the L.A. Summer Olympics, we outfitted our Olympic team in snazzy red, white and blue musical revue costumes—other countries chose dignified two-piece suits. Our team bopped into the stadium wearing sequined sunglasses shaped like hearts—other teams walked into the stadium in solemn procession."

"What's your point, Jess?"

Jessica rested her palms on the desk and leaned toward him. "My point is, this is the soda pop generation, and I intend to cash in. In my opinion, we'd be negligent if we didn't give our client an innovative campaign. A campaign full of life and energy, as full of life and energy as our society. I refuse to be negligent."

Clay stood, stretched, then faced her. His posture was relaxed, but his eyes sparkled with determination. "Good ploy, but I still don't buy it." He cocked his head to one side and scratched his beard. "I think you want to knock your father out with both a big bucks and big awards campaign. A campaign doesn't have to be new or slick to be a winner. Let's face it, in advertising a winner's a seller."

Placing her fists on her hips, she glared at him. Pulling her father into this was both unfair and way off base. If he was going to play dirty, so was she. "And I think you're lazy. Too lazy to do the extra creative work involved in coming up with an innovative campaign. You're trying to take the easy way out."

"Are we name calling . . . Jess?"

She tilted her chin. "You tell me . . . Clayton."

"Clay."

"Jessica." She tossed her head. "And you started it."

"Well now, that's logical and mature," he drawled sarcastically. "Logical, practical Jessica. You surprise me."

Jessica knew her cheeks were flushed. It infuriated her that he could almost provoke her to toss professionalism to the winds and descend to name-calling. She took a deep, calming breath. "Would you have me be illogical, impractical, immature?"

Her inference was clear, and Clay's eyes met hers in challenge. "But are you always practical? Don't you ever do anything just because?"

"Why would I want to?" she shot back, her eyes traveling over him impudently. "I believe there's always a reason for an action. A practical, logical reason. For me, just because doesn't cut it."

Clay silently regarded her. She was so elegant. So cool. Her blond hair was pulled away from her face and into a neat coil at her nape. There wasn't a wrinkle in her oyster-colored linen suit and her cosmetics were subtly blended.

She was too perfect, too composed. He wanted to see her hair tangled, her clothes rumpled. He wanted to see her eyes sparkle, her cheeks flush. A hint of a smile curved the corners of his mouth. This woman admired control, placed merit on calm. Drawing emotion from her was going to be a pleasure.

"If you rule your life with logic, if you're always practical, where's the surprise?" Clay's voice was even. "Where's the excitement? The challenge?"

"That's the difference between us—" her eyes flicked over him "—and shows in our respective choices of campaign styles. I find my work a constant challenge. And exciting. And full of surprises."

Clay's gaze locked with hers. "How about sex . . . Jess?"

Ignoring the way her stomach flip-flopped, she lifted a delicate eyebrow. "No thank you, you're not my type."

As she turned away, Clay grabbed her hand and swung her around. He'd wanted to needle her, but instead found himself needled. "Would agreeing to make love with me be the result of a practical, logical decision?"

Jessica glared at him. "Of course."

"And I prefer fire to ice. I'm not a masochist—I have no desire for freezer burn."

Fire exploded in her eyes; her cheeks flushed with anger. "And I told you, you're not my type. I don't make love with bums or hairy barbarians. Now let go of my hand." She tugged against his grasp.

"Oh no?" He tightened his hand over hers and began to rhythmically stroke the underside of her wrist. Their eyes met. "I could turn you to fire."

"Don't flatter yourself." Fury curled through her, scrambling her pulse, raising her temperature.

"We barbarians know how to conquer and melt ice princesses." He lowered his voice to a husky murmur. "I could conquer you, Jess."

"You're insane," Jessica whispered, lowering her eyes to where their flesh met. Tan against ivory, strong against smooth. She caught her bottom lip in her teeth. His hand was beautifully shaped. The fingers were long and blunt, the nails closely clipped and meticulously clean. She was startled by the incongruity between the man and his hands. He dressed like a barbarian, acted like a lunatic—and had the hands of a poet.

There was a sprinkling of blond hair on the back of his hand, and she suddenly wanted to trail her finger over it to discover if it was as soft as it looked. Jessica lifted her eyes in surprise. His were pinned on her, dark with awareness. For a moment Jessica allowed herself to be sucked into that blue gaze, filled with the promise of excitement, the promise of warmth.

And the promise of the loss of reason. The truth of that ripped through her like buckshot. What was she doing? The man was crazy, she was crazy. This was ridiculous. . . . She jerked her hand from his grasp and spun away.

Clay let her go. He'd surprised her and, in the process, surprised himself. He was an honest man; touching her had been a pleasure. His blood had raced, his senses had swum with her scent, her softness, her person.

As he knew hers had raced and swum. She'd responded to him with the same stunning force—he'd seen it in the fear that shot into her eyes a moment before she'd turned away. He didn't know why he reacted so strongly to touching her; he didn't care. There wasn't any sense in approaching the illogical with logic, the emotional with intellect. No, he preferred just to enjoy, to savor the unexpected gift.

Clay stared at her stiff spine and squared shoulders. The ice princess was back. Although she would never admit it, for a moment she'd been alive with fire. "What are we going to do, Jess?" Clay asked softly.

She swung around. Her heart was still racing, but her features remained coolly composed. "About what?"

His eyes swept slowly over her before settling on the pulse that was throbbing in her neck—there was the certainty. His smile was broad and satisfied. "The campaign, of course."

"Of course," Jessica repeated, reaching up to smooth her hair. When she caught the nervous gesture, she silently swore and dropped her hand. After a moment her eyes met his. "You know my position, Clay. And I'm not budging."

"Neither am I."

Jessica glared at him. Stubborn. He was like a dog with a bone—he just wouldn't let go. Surely he could see hers was the better direction? Frustrated, she let her breath out in a silent puff of air. "We have to come to an agreement."

"Yes." Clay stared out the window, absorbed in thought. After a moment he turned back toward her. "Why don't we let the clients decide?" he proposed slowly.

Jessica's brow furrowed, then cleared. "Work up each direction, then present them with both?" She nodded. "I like the idea, but it'll mean a lot of extra work."

"I'm up for it."

"So am I." Jessica held out her hand. "May the best campaign take it all."

"Yes, indeed." Clay took her hand. "Let the games begin."

Jessica tipped her head and nudged one of the two origami figures with her forefinger. It was either a fat dog or a short cow. Whichever it was, it was kind of cute and not a bad job considering all Clay had had to work with was two slightly used napkins.

Jessica scowled and set the tiny sculptures aside. She'd spent the week trying to reason away what had happened between Clay and her. It hadn't made any sense, it wasn't logical. And every time she'd come to that conclusion, she'd also become furious.

Everything had a logical explanation; she just hadn't ferreted this one out yet. Jessica stood and walked to the window. Clay wasn't helping any. They hadn't spoken since Tuesday morning—which was fine with her—but running into each other was unavoidable. Whenever they passed, he'd just look at her and smile.

The smile was a classic Mona Lisa. It tilted only slightly and said nothing or everything, depending on your point of view. Infuriating and annoying, she thought as she stared at the traffic jam thirty floors below.

The expression in his eyes was just as maddening. It wasn't friendly, but it wasn't unfriendly either. It was oblique and compelling, neutral and intimate. The hairy, disreputable beast! What was he thinking?

Not that she cared, of course. Jessica's scowl deepened, and she returned to her desk. She wasn't the least bit put off that she had to meet with the infuriating man this morning. Picking up the phone, she rang Barbara.

"Barbara, find Clay and tell him I need to see him immediately."

"Sure, Jess—er, Jessica. Right away."

"Thank you." Jessica replaced the receiver and silently swore; he had the whole office calling her that stupid nickname. She absently rubbed her temples.

"Headache, Jess?"

She lifted her eyes and scowled.

"You work, worry and frown too much. That's why you get headaches." Clay sauntered into her office and lowered himself into the chair opposite her. "And I already warned you about wrinkles. You need to relax. Learn to take it easy and enjoy yourself."

Her eyes flicked insultingly over him. "Like you?"

"Sure." He flashed her his most disarming smile. "You could model your life after mine. I won't mind. Imitation is the sincerest form of flattery."

"I'd sooner eat spoiled meat," Jessica muttered; she couldn't help herself. Then she took a deep breath and promised herself to keep this meeting on a professional level. Or die trying, she thought grimly. "How are you coming with your designs?"

"Just fine, princess. How are you coming on yours?"

She would stay calm, she would stay cool. "Sandra Miller called."

"Oh?"

He was doing it again. Staring at her with that blank but knowing expression, the jerk. "She and her brother have decided to redesign the thirty-four cookie stores to fit the look of the advertising campaign."

"Mmm-hmm."

What did that mean? He was trying to unnerve her, she was sure of it. Why? She didn't care, she would just ignore him. Jessica picked up a pencil and tapped it against her palm. "They'd like us to become familiar with their stores so we can make suggestions concerning the interiors when we deliver the advertising package. Sandra suggested we visit the Laguna Beach store. It was their first and is representative of the others. They'd also like us to recommend a space planner. I intend to recommend my sister Alicia along with several others. If you have anyone in mind, have Barbara add them to my list."

He hadn't blinked, not once, since sitting down. Jessica tightened her fingers on the pencil. "You're doing it again. Stop it."

Clay lifted his eyebrows. "Doing what?"

The pencil snapped in two. "Staring at me as if I'm an insect under a glass or a strange form of plant life." Jessica glared at him. "You've been doing it all week."

"Have I?"

"Yes, you have."

Clay grinned and leaned back in his seat. "You must have been staring at me to know I've been staring at you."

"What!" Jessica pressed her palms to her forehead. "Never mind, Clay. I just want you to stop it. You're driving me crazy."

"See."

"See what, for God's sake? No!" Jessica held out a hand to hold off his reply. "No more talking in circles, no more answering my questions with questions." She jumped up and began to pace. "You're illogical and impractical and unprofessional. And you're making me that way." She swung around to face him. "I won't have it. Do you hear me, Clay? I won't have it." The phone rang; she didn't answer, but waited instead for his reply.

Her cheeks were flushed with color, her eyes sparkled like water in the sun. Satisfied, Clay shrugged and smiled. "Sure, Jess. Whatever you say."

"Thank you," she returned stiffly, then turned to pick up the phone. "Jessica Mann."

As she picked up the phone Clay's eyes drifted to the window, then snapped back to her when she greeted someone named John. Her voice warmed and a smile touched her lips as she did so. John? Who the hell was John?

"That would be lovely. What time?" She jotted the information on her notepad, laughed and said goodbye.

Not only did he want to know who this John was, he wanted to know how he got Jessica to laugh and smile. Clay's eyes glinted with determination. "Who was that?" he asked, eyeing the notepad.

"A friend. Now—"

"John?"

"Yes." She perched on the edge of her desk. "Let's get back to the problem at hand."

"Do I know him?"

Jessica made a frustrated sound. "I don't think so. How should I know? Why?"

"Maybe I'm just a curious guy." Clay shrugged. "When do you propose we go to Laguna?"

Jessica picked up her calendar. "That's problematic. I'm booked solid next week, and the first part of the week after. I hate to put this off, but the trip will take an entire day—"

"How about the weekend?"

Jessica flipped through the book. "This weekend is out. I'm meeting with our tax attorney tomorrow and have to catch up on paperwork Sunday. If it's good for you, I can schedule it for next weekend."

Clay smiled. This was the opening he'd been waiting for. "Let me write down those dates." She handed him the notepad and a pen. He jotted them down and said, "I don't think there'll be a conflict, but I'll check my calendar and get back to you."

"Fine." Jessica stood and walked him to the door. "Let me know by Monday."

"No problem." He grinned and backed away, moving down the hall. "See you real soon, Jess." His grin widened as she scowled at him before returning to her office.

"Evening. Whatever you have on tap will be fine." Clay laid a five on the bar and glanced at his watch. Six-twenty; she would be here soon. He was prying; he knew it, but felt no guilt. He'd wanted to see her outside the office, had wanted a glimpse of her private side.

He tapped a quarter against the cool marble bar. He wasn't sure why he was so interested. Maybe it was because they had to work together and he wanted to understand her.... No, that wasn't it. Maybe he was just curious. He was just a curious, friendly guy. He took a long swallow of the draft and shook his head. That was bull. He knew many people on a strictly professional level and had never followed them on a date. So, what was it about this woman that turned him into a nosey old busybody? Disgusted with himself, Clay glanced at the doorway.

Her dress was of orange silk and subtly patterned. The shoulders were padded, the skirt was straight. It skimmed her body as she moved, and he was fascinated by the ripple of light on the shiny fabric. Pearls glimmered at her ears, throat and wrist, and Clay knew they were genuine. She was a woman who would wear real pearls or no pearls at all.

Maybe it was the way she carried herself, Clay thought, cocking his head and running his hand along his clean-shaven jaw. Erectly and smoothly. He'd never seen her slouch and suspected he never would.

Maybe it was her untouchable, unflappable class. Or her cool facade. Or the way she arched her delicate eyebrows in question or outrage. Maybe it was her infrequent smiles and the way they lit her face like the sun peeking out from behind a cloud.

Authenticity. His eyes roamed over her. In a world of plastic values and paper sunsets, of mood lighting and imitation everything, she was the real thing. She didn't pretend, didn't have to try. He grinned into his beer. She was either an authentic princess or he'd been in advertising too long. Clay downed the last swallow and motioned to the bartender for another.

Ali did a great job, Jessica thought, glancing around the crowded bar. The room was intimate because of her sister's design rather than its size. The interior was crowded with plants and patterns, the lighting was soft and warm, the piped-in music subdued. *Little sister has come of age,* Jessica decided, a soft smile touching her lips.

She'd chosen a table almost obscured by plants. The choice wasn't made, as many would assume, so she could be alone with a lover, but because she enjoyed privacy in public places. There was an ambiguity in that that appealed to her.

Jessica glanced at her watch; John was late. Some last-minute crisis at the bank, she thought, her eyes skimming the room. They rested on a man at the bar, moved on, then returned to him. A slight frown settled on her brow. Who was that? She knew, but couldn't place him. Curious, her gaze flicked over him again. The way he held himself—with relaxed poise, like a man who was comfortable with himself—was familiar. The tilt of the head, the way he gestured with his hands . . .

She caught her breath. It couldn't be, could it? She strained to see him more clearly. Just then, the man swung around and looked at her. Their eyes tangled. His were unmistakable. It was Clay. A clean-shaven and respectably dressed Clay.

She swore softly as he smiled and stood up. Jessica realized her palms were sweating and cursed again. She was acting irrationally and didn't like it. Determined to remain calm, she sipped her mineral water and breathed deeply.

Clay picked up his beer and headed across the room. This was all wrong, he told himself. It was an intrusion; it was unforgivable. He was a spy on a fact-finding mission—he grinned at that—and he hadn't planned to approach her. But he wanted to, so that would just have to be good enough.

"Hello, Jess." She had the smoothest skin he'd ever seen. A trick of the light, he assured himself, even as his gaze lingered on the curve of her jaw.

She tipped her head to look up at him, her neck arching with the movement. "Hello, Clay." Jessica had to admit he looked nice. He'd substituted his usual jeans and T-shirt for khaki-colored, pleated trousers and a red cotton sweater. The sleeves were pushed up to his elbows and Jessica found herself staring at his muscular forearms.

"May I join you?" His eyes roamed down the line of her throat, enticed by the sensual arc.

"Yes." The word came out as a husky invitation. Annoyed, she cleared her throat and repeated the affirmative. "Yes, of course."

Setting his beer on the table, he straddled the chair across from her. "So, do you come here often?"

Startled by the change in his appearance, she stared at him. He had a beautiful face. No, she amended, it was too rugged to be beautiful. She tilted her head to one side. And it was better than nice. Much better. Dimples and laughing eyes kept it from being rakish, chiseled features and sweeping eyebrows made cuteness an impossibility. An interesting face, a compelling one.

He'd cut his hair. Short on the top and sides, it curled against his neck in back. It looked soft and was the color of raw honey. She found herself wanting to touch it.

He crossed his arms and cocked his head. "Do I pass muster, Jess?"

Her eyes flew to his and heat tinted her cheeks. She tossed her head. "Well, you're not hairy anymore."

He laughed. "I'm overwhelmed, Jessica." Placing his chin on his fist, he grinned at her. "But am I still a bum?"

"Of course." She averted her eyes to hide the amusement in them. "Am I still a prissy princess?"

"In that dress?" He lowered his eyes to the swell of her breasts, softly draped in silk. "You look wonderful," he murmured.

Her lips curved, her pulse fluttered. "What brings you here?"

"Truthfully?"

"Mmm."

"Truthfully, I don't know." He took a long swallow of beer. "I was trying to figure that out when our eyes met. How about you?"

She trailed her finger along the moisture-beaded glass. "I'm meeting someone."

"John?"

"Yes. How did you know?"

Clay gestured with his fingers. "Your office the other day. He called."

"Oh." She sipped her drink; silence stretched between them.

Clay finished his beer. "He's late."

"Yes."

"Don't you mind?"

She shrugged. "No. Should I?"

"Not my business, Jess."

She raised an eyebrow. "Has that ever stopped you before?"

"No. But then, I don't like to disappoint people." He bit back a smile. "So, where is he?"

"I don't know. How should I know?" She made a frustrated noise. "Don't look at me like that. He's not standing me up. He's a busy man. He got tied up, that's all." Jessica glanced hopefully toward the doorway, then smiled in relief. "There he is. I told you he wasn't standing me up."

"Where?" Clay craned his neck in the direction she'd indicated.

"There, in the navy pin-striped suit."

"Not the old guy who looks like a banker."

Jessica's spine stiffened. "He's not old, and what's wrong with the banking profession?"

"Not old? He's ancient." Clay turned back to her, doing his best to look both sincere and shocked. "What is he, twenty, twenty-five years your senior?"

Jessica gasped. "He's only forty-two. There's only twelve years between us and—"

Clay's eyes widened. "Gee, it must be banking that's made him age prematurely. Such a stodgy, pretentious profession." His tone became gossipy as he leaned toward her and wiggled his eyebrows. "I'll bet he wears wing tips."

"Stop it!" Jessica glared at him; her hands were shaking so she folded them in her lap. "He's a nice man."

Clay jumped on the adjective. "Nice? Is that what you look for in a man?"

"Of course," she snapped, annoyance curling through her. Who was he to question her private choices? "What should I look for?'' she asked icily. ''Hairy barbarians? Disreputable bums?''

''Sure, why not?'' Clay jerked his head toward her date, who'd stopped to talk to a couple at the bar. ''It'd beat the hell out of stodgy old geezers who wear wing tip shoes.''

''You're insufferable,'' Jessica said through gritted teeth.

''Now I know why you don't mind if he's late.'' Clay stood up. ''Because being alone is just as exciting as his company. Maybe more so.''

''You know nothing about me,'' she flung back, standing to face him. ''How would you know what excites me?''

''I know this....'' Abruptly Clay hauled her against his chest. His eyes captured hers as he held her possessively. ''I could excite you, Jess. I could make it so that every minute I was late you would tremble with the anticipation of my touch.''

Jessica's breath caught, her pulse points tingled. ''You think so, do you?'' Her voice was an unrecognizable whisper, breathy and totally feminine.

''I know so.'' He softly stroked the pulse that was throbbing behind her ear. ''I could turn you to fire.''

''You're arrogant and conceited,'' she whispered, words her only defense against the languor stealing over her.

''Thank you,'' he murmured, his breath mingling with hers. ''You'll never call me nice, Jess.'' He lowered his mouth to capture hers. Her lips were warm and tasted slightly of citrus and Perrier. The combination was delicious, and he pressed closer, sampling her flavors with his tongue. Her scent was heady, not quite floral and not quite musk. Clay breathed deeply, letting it fill and surround him.

A moan caught in her throat as her lips yielded to his. He hadn't surprised her; she'd meant to resist. But his kiss stole over her the way the sun stole over the horizon, slowly and brilliantly. And suddenly, like a new day, she felt alive with light and heat. And freedom, an intoxicating, overwhelming freedom. Dizzy with the sensations that were rollercoastering through her, she curled her fingers into his sweater.

Clay pulled away, surprised by the way he needed her, surprised by the way she'd responded to him. This hadn't been an ordinary kiss, but then she wasn't an ordinary woman. Clay drank in her beauty with a hunger and greed that stunned him. Giving in to that greed, he lowered his head once more. Her lips were moist and already parted; the contact was brief but shattering.

Aware that at any moment her date would find their private oasis, aware that five minutes from now she would be furious, he released her. As he did she swayed toward him, and he caressed her cheek with his fingertips. "Your date," he whispered.

"Yes." Disoriented, her eyes searched his. Reality began to intrude, and she relaxed her fingers against his chest, heat climbing into her cheeks.

He felt her stiffen before she actually did so, sensed her dismay before it raced into her eyes. He leaned toward her. "Remember this...." His breath stirred the wisps of hair that framed her face. "I'd never keep you waiting, Jessica. Never."

Three

The cup rattled against the saucer as she carried it to the sink. Jessica cursed her nerves. It was ridiculous, really. She absently rinsed the cup. He'd kissed her, just a simple kiss one week and one day ago.

Jessica frowned and dried her hands. It hadn't been a simple kiss; she'd thought she was going to die with delight, and there'd been nothing since. Nothing, she thought sourly, nothing but a smile, a wave, a "Good morning."

Which was fine with her. She tossed the towel onto the counter and stalked to the bedroom. He was crazy and unpredictable and had no place in her life. She didn't even like him—did she? She peeled off her robe. No, certainly not. After all, to like someone you had to respect them, and she didn't respect Clay Jones. He was unprofessional and, well...wacky.

He lingered in her thoughts only because she was still furious with him, Jessica assured herself. She had a right to be furious; he'd ruined her date and embarrassed her in public. She'd spent the whole evening apologizing and trying to explain. Poor old John had been scandalized and—

What was she thinking? Jessica caught her lower lip in her teeth and sank to the bed. Now she was doing it, calling John old and stodgy. So what if he wore wing tip shoes? So what if he was a member of the most conservative profession known to man? Did that prove he was a boring old geezer?

Moaning, she pressed the heels of her hands to her eyes; she was going crazy. Clay had wormed his way into her brain like cheap wine and unbalanced her. In the past week she'd caught herself staring stupidly into space, saying things that weren't pertinent to the conversation at hand and laughing for no reason at all. She was dizzy and lightheaded and pushed to the breaking point.

She squared her shoulders and took a deep breath. If she gave in to Clay's madness she would lose everything she'd worked for: her position at the agency, her father's growing respect, her future as a force in the advertising community.

Jessica tossed her head and marched to the closet. She'd come up against tougher obstacles, bigger distractions and won. Clay Jones would not break her; she simply wouldn't allow it. With a practiced eye, she scanned the contents of her closet, settling on a nubby linen skirt and matching short jacket. The short-sleeved blouse was also beige, but with an understated floral pattern throughout. Businesslike but sporty—perfect for a Saturday meeting.

Jessica checked her watch and cursed her second cup of coffee. She didn't have much time; Clay would be arriving any minute. She ignored the way her pulse scrambled at the thought, ignored the way she peered at her reflection and worried over her cosmetics. Just as she finished French-braiding her hair, she heard him at the door.

Jessica took a deep, calming breath and crossed the room. He'd ignored the bell and knocked, using the opportunity to be irreverent, as usual. He'd knocked in the same pattern children favor—five quick, unevenly spaced beats with a pause before finishing with two more quick beats. She rolled her eyes as she swung open the door; some children never grew up.

He was leaning against the doorjamb, his hands shoved into the pockets of faded black jeans. The sleeves of the white oxford shirt were rolled up to his elbows, the collar was open at the throat. He looked relaxed and confident, and Jessica found herself unreasonably annoyed. "I'm ready," she announced curtly. "Just let me grab my purse."

"Well, hello to you, too." Clay propelled himself away from the door and looked at her dubiously. "Are you sure? I mean, are you going dressed like that?"

Jessica glanced down at herself, then glared at him. "Like what?"

"Like that." Clay gestured vaguely at her outfit.

"Are you going dressed like that?" Jessica countered.

"This is Saturday," Clay said easily.

"This is business."

"Suit yourself, Jess."

"Thank you, I will."

Clay grinned at her stiff back and squared shoulders as she turned to lock the door. "We've got a beautiful day for the trip," he commented as they walked outside.

"Mmm." Jessica squinted at the sun. "Where's your car?" The only thing parked in front of her condominium was a large, black motorcycle.

"I don't have a car."

"But you said you'd drive."

"I did and I will." He pulled a set of keys from his pocket and walked to the bike.

Jessica stopped, horrified. "Not that?"

"Yeah." Clay ran a gentle hand over the seat. "Isn't she a beauty?"

"No, she's not." Jessica placed her fists on her hips. "I'm not riding on that."

"Not in that skinny skirt you're not. Although..." He let the words trail off suggestively as his eyes skimmed the length of her legs. "Don't worry, I have two helmets."

"I can't believe you didn't tell me...I can't believe... A motorcycle?" She lifted despairing eyes from the bike to Clay.

He shrugged. "Sorry. I didn't think it was a big deal."

"Not a big deal? Look at the way I'm dressed! We're talking about a two-hour drive, not a trip to the market. A two-hour drive on the highway. Besides that, this is business and...and..." She groaned loudly in frustration, then whirled around and headed back inside.

Clay followed her. "If it's a problem, why don't you drive?"

Jessica jammed the key into the lock after tossing him a furious glance. "My Volvo's in the shop being tuned up; I didn't think I'd need it today."

Clay tried to hold back the laugh, but couldn't. "Volvo? You drive a Volvo?" He grinned at her. "Why aren't I surprised?"

"Volvos are good cars," Jessica said defensively. "They're..."

"Sensible, practical, staid," Clay supplied, the grin widening.

"Yes!" She glared at him. "I can't think of a better reason to buy a car."

"They last forever—kinda like wing tip shoes."

She wanted to scream, wanted to hit him. Jessica assured herself that she would do neither. She counted to ten, took a deep breath, then said through clenched teeth, "You enjoy doing this, don't you?"

"What?" Clay was the picture of boyish innocence.

"Driving me crazy, raising my blood pressure, making my life a living hell."

"Do I do that?" He reached out and gently touched her flushed cheek with his index finger. "At least you're not immune to my charms."

She told herself to pull away from his touch, but didn't move. "You're an impossible jerk."

"I'm sorry...." At her disbelieving expression, he hastened to add, "No, really I am. I don't know why I goad you." His grin was sheepish. "Part of it is you get so riled.... I can't help myself."

Jessica stepped away from his caressing hand. "I'm glad you're having a good time at my expense. I live to be the butt of your stupid jokes. Really, I do. Now, if you'll excuse me, I'm going to change." What had she expected from him—sonnets? She headed for the bedroom.

"Whoa." Clay grabbed her arm and pulled her back. "Let me finish."

She opened her mouth to retort; the look in his eyes stopped her. They were soft with regret. Swallowing her anger, she gave him a chance.

"You're always in control, always so cool, so perfect. I sense that you store your emotions like a squirrel stores nuts for the winter. I like making you break into your stash, Jess. I like your anger, your smile...." He cupped her face with his hands. "Your laughter."

"Why?" she asked softly. "Why can't you accept me as I am? Serious, practical Jessica...that's who I am, Clay."

"Because..." He turned his back to her, running a hand through his already rumpled hair in frustration. "I don't know why." He swung back toward her. "Maybe I think it's a lie. Maybe I think there's another Jessica inside, a silly, impractical, emotional Jessica."

"There's not, Clay. This is it, the whole package." She held out her hands, palms up. "Serious, practical, steady. If I were a man I'd wear wing tip shoes."

"And be a banker?" Clay's expression was dubious.

"Definitely."

Clay shoved his hands into his pockets and rocked back on his heels. "I don't buy it."

"Too bad, because you don't have—" She shook her head, then laughed. "We're doing it again. What is it with us, Clay? We'll never agree on anything, will we?"

"Mmm...maybe not." Clay grinned suddenly. "I've got an idea. Let's agree to agree. We'll make it a contest, a game."

She tapped her chin and cocked her head as if contemplating the universe. "Hmm... I don't know. What are the rules?"

"We'll agree to agree for today only. Twenty-four hours of peace, equanimity, goodwill toward one another. Do you agree?"

Jessica's eyes sparkled. "How could I not?" She held out her hand. "It's a deal then. No arguing, no picking, no teasing."

He took her hand. "Twenty-four hours. First person to disagree buys dinner."

"You got it, Jones." She tossed her head; her eyes narrowed. "But I'm warning you, I'm a fierce competitor. You'll collapse like a house of cards, I guarantee it."

Clay threw back his head and laughed. "I'm not going to disagree with that."

An hour and a half later, he swung off the bike and grinned at Jessica. "See, that wasn't so bad."

Jessica glared at him as she jerked off the heavy helmet. She lifted her face to the breeze, letting it cool her sweat-dampened head. Without turning she said, "No, it wasn't so bad. So what if several of my vital organs have moved to a new location! Everything deserves a change of scenery. So what if my teeth need caps; I like my dentist, he needs to make a living. So what if I'll never bear children—"

Laughing, Clay held up his hands. "Please, no more! I'm already riddled with guilt."

"Mmm, I'm sure." Jessica slanted him an amused glance.

"Really." He draped an arm over her shoulders and they began to walk. "I can prove it."

"Oh?" Clay's masculine scent teased her senses and Jessica steeled herself against the urge to snuggle into his chest.

"Yeah. I'll pick up the tab for some cookies."

"Oh, well, that certainly makes up for the inability to bear children," Jessica teased back.

"I thought so." He gave her shoulders a quick squeeze, then dropped his arm. "Here we are. After you, Madam Vice-President." He pushed open the glass door that announced Cookies from Heaven in bright blue letters, then bowed. Grinning, Jessica sashayed by him, unaware of the way his eyes followed the movement of her hips.

The interior of the shop was clean, serviceable and impersonal. Jessica ran practiced eyes over the room, noting and assessing every detail. There was nothing about it to make it unique or inviting. The counters were white Formica, the glass display cases were filled with trays of cookies, the walls were papered white with red pinstripe. The space possessed a wealth of possibilities; all it needed was direction.

"The cookies must be from heaven," Clay whispered in her ear. "The interior certainly isn't bringing in any customers."

"No kidding," Jessica shot back.

The young woman behind the counter, a beautiful blonde who openly flirted with Clay, was helpful and friendly. A little too helpful and friendly, Jessica thought sourly as the girl flashed Clay a provocative look. She wasn't jealous, Jessica assured herself. Why would she be jealous of a twenty-year-old with big breasts, long legs and a great tan? Ridiculous. Besides, it was necessary to care about and be possessive of someone to be jealous. And that wasn't the case. Not at all. She just didn't approve of all those come-hither looks and sexy smiles in public.

Color crept into her cheeks as she saw the buxom blonde slide Clay her phone number along with his change. Jessica silently groaned as she realized she wanted to slap the girl silly. This wasn't going well. She'd promised herself she would remain cool and collected—was wanting to slap an innocent bystander silly acting cool and collected? She thought not. It was crazy and neurotic. Her heart sank. All this over a man she didn't even like.

"Jess? Jess . . . you ready?"

"What?" She lifted her eyes in surprise and followed him out the door. Heat washed over her as she realized she'd been staring at his, well . . . hip region. "Oh, yes. I was just thinking about the . . . the campaign," she improvised.

"Of course." Clay's eyes crinkled at the corners, but he didn't comment on the color in her cheeks or her obvious confusion. "How about taking the goodies down to the beach?"

"Just what goodies are you referring to?" Jessica asked, tipping her head to meet his eyes.

Clay shook the bag. "The cookies, of course. What else?"

She sniffed. "I thought maybe you meant Miss-oh-so-bold's goodies."

"Jessica!" Clay pretended to look shocked, then burst out laughing. "Tsk, tsk. Jessica, have you been touched by the green-eyed ghoul?"

"Ridiculous." She shot him an amused glance as she slung her purse over her shoulder. "Just making an observation about your taste in women. I've always preferred brains to beauty myself."

Clay arched an eyebrow. "Meaning she didn't have any?"

"She was flirting with *you*, wasn't she?" Jessica's expression was smug.

"Touché." He fitted his stride to hers. "But I had to be nice. Would you have wanted me to hurt her feelings?"

Jessica rolled her eyes. "Of course not."

"Hey, I'm being sincere here." His dimples appeared. "I'm a sensitive, empathetic guy."

"Oh, sure. A sensitive barbarian. A..." Jessica stopped, grabbed his arm and pointed. Her words rushed out on a sigh. "Look, isn't it beautiful." The sun had escaped from behind the cloud cover and radiated off the ocean like laser beams hitting the fragments of a billion shattered mirrors. "It makes man's attempts at beauty seem rather petty, doesn't it?"

"Yes," Clay murmured, his gaze fixed on her face. Her expression was that of a poet, a romantic. The eyes he'd once thought icy were fathomless pools of dreams, the lips he'd once thought mean were moist and softly parted. Her golden hair caught the sun and shimmered like blond fire. He frowned. She was a woman of contradictions, not the woman she proclaimed herself to be. But he was a man who liked contradictions, and who liked surprises most of all.

He should leave her alone, Clay thought, suddenly frustrated. He should ignore his desire to strip away her layers of protection to find the woman beneath. Because once he found her he was afraid he would be unable to let her go. And she wasn't good for him.

He drew a sharp breath. Maybe the very reasons he should stay away from her were what drew her to him. His stomach tightened at the thought. He couldn't allow—

"How about stopping here?" Jessica asked. "It seems like a nice spot."

Clay jerked his thoughts back to the present. She'd sunk to the sand and pulled her knees up to her chest. Her smile was relaxed and easy as she stared out at the water. She was so beautiful. He wanted to kiss her until she melted against him, until they both forgot who they were and why being together was all wrong.

"What kind did you buy for us to sample?" she asked, grinning up at him.

It was the grin that did it. Shelving his worries, he sat down beside her. "All of them."

"All?" She grabbed the bag and peeked inside. Her eyes were laughing as they met his. "Whatever for?"

Clay dimpled. "To effectively build Cookies from Heaven's campaign we need to be thoroughly familiar with their product. I mean, how could we do their advertising if we'd never tasted the chocolate cookie with the peanut butter chips?"

"Or the peanut butter cookie with the chocolate chips. That's a hint by the way."

"Right." He handed her the requested cookie and a napkin. "I bought you milk to drink. Hope you don't mind."

"Low fat?"

"Of course."

"Perfect." She took a bite of the cookie and moaned with pleasure. "They *are* from heaven. Only God could make cookies this good." She took another bite, savoring its flavor against her tongue. "I love peanut butter. And chocolate."

"The power of advertising. The peanut butter cup jingle is running through my head." Clay grinned, reaching for another. "Were you a peanut butter and jelly kid?"

"Still am. But worse—" she leaned toward him "—I'm a sugar junkie."

"No?"

"Yes." Her eyes danced with humor. "And a chocoholic."

"I never would have guessed it," he teased. "Sensible, staid Jessica a sweet addict."

"Mmm." She fished around in the bag, then pulled out a chocolate and butterscotch cookie. "I've never drowned my sorrows with liquor. I've bathed them in sugar."

"Tacky."

"And fattening." They stared at each other a moment, lips twitching, then burst out laughing. Jessica laughed so hard that her eyes ran and her middle hurt. Holding her stomach she flopped onto the sand, her laughter abating into uncharacteristic giggles. Wiping her eyes she said, "The clouds look like chubby cotton balls and Greek gods."

"That's quite a combination." Clay propped himself on an elbow and looked down at her. "I like you this way, Jessica."

She pulled her eyes from the puffy, white formations and glanced at him from the corner of her eyes. "What way?"

"Soft and silly." He touched her cheek lightly, just once, with his index finger. "Carefree."

Her eyes returned to the clouds. "I don't have time to be silly and carefree. I have an agency to run. A career to build."

"How about soft, Jess?"

She met his eyes again. "A woman in business can't afford to be vulnerable, Clay."

"I said soft, not vulnerable." Her eyes were as clear and blue as a morning sky. Clay knew he could lose himself in them. "They're not the same thing."

"In business they are. Soft is perceived as weak. Only the strong make it to the executive ranks; most women are trampled along the way." Her eyes challenged. "I wasn't and won't be."

"Strong, dependable, responsible. Good traits, Jessica. But not to the exclusion of all others." He absently toyed with the wisps of hair that had escaped her braid and were framing her face. They felt like down against his fingers. "It's okay to be vulnerable sometimes. It's okay to be soft."

She smiled. "Are you disagreeing with me?"

His eyes searched her face, his lips curved. "I believe I am."

"Well then, Jones, you must pay the consequences. You've lost the game. The dinner is mine." She stood, brushed off the seat of her pants, and held a hand out to him.

Grinning, Clay clasped it and propelled himself up, then catching her off guard, tumbled her into his arms.

A surprised gasp caught in her throat as she landed against Clay's chest. His heart beat wildly under her palm, and she lifted her eyes to his.

"It's funny, Jess."

His warm breath mingled with hers. "What is?"

"Right now I don't feel like I lost anything." He tightened his arms around her. "In fact, I feel like a winner. A big winner."

"Oh?" The word was a husky imitation of her voice.

"Mmm-hmm." He lowered his head. "Now for the grand prize..."

Jessica ran her hands up his chest as his mouth found hers. It wasn't a teasing kiss, it wasn't coy. His lips seduced hers, demanded response. And she gave to him, emptying her mind of everything but his flavor, his touch. This was what she'd wanted, what she'd needed since the last time he'd touched her. This freedom. This intoxication. Curling her fingers into his hair, she deepened the kiss.

Chocolate lingered on her tongue and Clay wanted more, wanted to go deeper, to drink in the nuance and subtlety that was Jessica. His tongue thrust and twined, promising to give as well as to receive.

Wrenching his mouth from hers, Clay found the pulse that was throbbing wildly, warmly in her throat. Her scent was almost overpowering there and he breathed in the heady fragrance, wondering if it would be the same at her elbows, behind her knees.

Jessica arched her neck; her lids fluttered open. As she did, the endless expanse of azure sky greeted her. It pulled at her, absorbed her. She floated, feeling as soft and insubstantial as the wisps of white above her, as vulnerable as the shore being constantly licked at by the greedy ocean.

She blinked. Clay was dangerous because he made her feel those things. Her life was carefully mapped out; there was no place for softness or vulnerability or crazy men who made her feel intoxicated.

Her body stiffened. The hands that had caressed now resisted. "No, Clay...stop."

"Aw, princess..." Clay rested his forehead against hers, breathing deeply, willing his body to relax. Willing away the ache in his loins. "You know I don't want to."

She drew in a deep, steadying breath. "Yes."

"But it's what you want." His eyes searched hers. "Isn't it?"

"Yes." She met his gaze evenly because it was what she wanted. Not with her heart, but with her intellect. With the Jessica she knew best—the Jessica she trusted. "And I don't want you to kiss me again."

"Not ever?" Clay's tone and expression were solemn.

"Not ever."

"Aw, Jess..." He wouldn't ask her why because he already knew. He also knew it wasn't over. He smiled brilliantly. "Wanna take a walk with me and talk cookies?"

She raised her eyebrows in surprise, unable to believe he wasn't going to push the issue. "That's it?"

"Yeah. Is there something else you'd like?"

Jessica flushed. "No, it's just that... No, nothing. A walk would be wonderful."

Laguna Beach was the quintessential California community. The property was pricey, the atmosphere relaxed, and the people were chic.

And it was absolutely beautiful. The coast undulated through the landscape like yards of lace attached to a flamboyant lamé dress. Foothills surrounded it all, nestling the beach community like a gold setting nestles a precious stone.

Even with all those things Jessica preferred Los Angeles. It was a big, dirty city with all the problems that come with that description. Things like crime and congestion and crazies. But there was an indefinable energy about the city, a magic that pumped through her system like information through a computer network. Just as she'd never wanted to be anything but the president of The Mann Agency, she'd never wanted to live anywhere else.

But Clay preferred the country, she thought, shooting him a glance as they turned down one of the narrow side streets. How else could he spend three months fishing in Wisconsin? She sighed. It was just another way they were different.

The street was lined with quaint shops and exclusive boutiques, and Jessica nudged her sunglasses back up her nose after stopping to inspect a pair of designer pumps in a store window. "You know, Clay, after seeing the Cookies from Heaven store I'm more convinced than ever that my direction is the perfect one. Imagine this—" she gestured with her hands as she spoke "—shiny black and white ceramic tile counters, nubby black Italian tile floors, shots of neon in hot colors, stools lining the counters finished in patent leather the same colors as the neon. Piped-in rock'n'roll, contemporary art on the walls. What do you think?"

"I think it sounds like a set from a slick TV show." When she didn't comment, Clay shot her an amused glance. "Am I going to get stuck with another dinner?"

"Well, I guess that answers my question," Jessica said on a sigh. "I was hoping to sway you."

"Life would be simpler." Clay considered putting an arm around her, then thought better of it. "Actually I like it. It's a funky version of what I had in mind—an old-fashioned ice-cream parlor interior. Maybe we can compromise?"

"No way, Jones. I'm holding out for the big victory." She stopped to peer into a craft store window before turning back to him. "Let's face it. We're both designing the space to fit our initial ideas which is the same thing the space planner will do." Jessica shoved her hands into her pockets in frustration. She'd really hoped he would come around. She was so sure her direction was the unequaled choice. "If you're not willing to budge—I'm not—we'll have to present both directions to the client as originally planned.''

"Yeah." He liked the way she was starting to purse her lips. It made him want to tease them with the tip of his tongue. He shrugged. "Life's like a bowl of cherries; sometimes it's the pits."

"My, my..." She clucked her tongue, her eyes twinkling. "A barbarian and a philosopher. Some people have it all."

He grinned, not at all offended by her words. "Yeah, isn't it great." He took her elbow, guided her across the street and into a small art gallery. "I've gotten several pieces here. They deal exclusively in contemporary California artists. And—" he bent to whisper in her ear "—their reputation is impeccable. Like yours, princess."

A rude word came to mind. Jessica bit it back. Tipping her head toward him, she smiled sweetly and murmured, "Why, thank you, Clay. I take that as a great compliment, coming from you."

"Bull," he said cheerfully.

Jessica removed her sunglasses as they stepped into the gallery. She was impressed with what she saw. The best Los Angeles galleries had nothing on this one. The arrangement of the artworks, the lighting and neutral colors of the interior were professional even by New York standards. She wandered in to get a closer look.

"Hey, Greg. How's biz?"

From the corner of one eye she saw Clay greet a man with longish, curly brown hair. Jessica almost choked when she heard Greg ask who the "cookie" was. Clay laughed, then said something about a "tempting morsel." *Macho jerks,* Jessica thought, gritting her teeth.

Her silent fuming was interrupted by an abstract landscape in oil. It wasn't a large painting, but seemed so because of its energy. The colors were bold, at times even garish, the frenzied brush strokes made those of Van Gogh look tame. She stood still, drinking in its surface, being absorbed by its life.

"Are you going to buy it?"

Even though Clay had whispered the question in her ear she jumped. She'd been so intent on the painting that the rest of the world had disappeared. "What?" She looked over her shoulder at him.

"Are you going to buy it?"

"No." She moved regretfully to the next work.

"I'll float you a loan. Or talk Greg into giving you credit." There was laughter in his voice. "He has a soft spot where 'cookies' are concerned."

"Hmm..." Jessica's eyes raked over him. "You two are a charming pair. Real quality guys."

Clay laughed, unaffected by her attempt to get his goat. "Well, how about it?"

"I have nowhere to put it."

Clay stuffed his hands into his pockets, rocking back on his heels. "Seems to me you have lots of places. Above the sofa, in the bathroom, behind your desk. How about the kitchen or bedroom?"

Jessica sighed. "I have plenty of space for it; it just doesn't go with any of my rooms. But this would." She stopped in front of the next painting, tipping her head to one side as she studied it. It was another abstract landscape, this time an interpretation of the ocean and sky. It was a lovely watercolor, done in neutral and pastel tones. "This is nice," Jessica murmured. "It would be lovely in my living room."

"I don't believe this!" Clay said incredulously, dragging a hand through his hair. "Do you even like it?"

"Of course I like it. I said it was nice, didn't I?"

"You're going to buy a painting just because it'll coordinate with your wallpaper and carpeting?"

Jessica tightened her lips and narrowed her eyes. "What better reason? I'm a businesswoman, Clay. I have to make practical, logical decisions on how to spend money every day. This is one of those decisions.''

"Like deciding to wear wing tip shoes or buy a Volvo?''

"That's it!'' She made a slicing gesture with her hands. "I'm through discussing this, Clay. I'm buying the painting.'' She swung around and headed for the back of the gallery.

Clay followed her. "This is the most illogical thing I've ever heard. You're going to buy a painting you only like and leave the painting you love.'' He grabbed her elbow. "Does that make sense? Does it?'' When she only glared at him he continued. "Art is about emotion, Jess. Art is about what calls out to an individual on a spiritual level. Choosing a piece of art isn't a cold-blooded business decision. It's warm, intimate.'' His voice lowered. "Like choosing a lover.''

"Let go of my arm.'' Her tone was furious. When she yanked on it he only tightened his grasp. Her eyes met his in challenge. "You know nothing about why or how I'd choose a lover. You never will.''

"Oh?'' Clay squelched the desire to prove her a liar and coolly lifted an eyebrow. "I think you'd choose a lover the same way you chose that painting. You want someone who'll go with your furniture. Neutral and tasteful and... nice. Like that stodgy old banker.''

Jessica clenched her hands in fury. "And what do you want? A woman with more breasts than brains? A woman who'll giggle when faced with an important decision? Or someone who'll accept your word and your views as law?''

He released her arm. "I don't want a woman whom I just like or think is nice. I want one who excites me—in every way. One who is open and emotional and warm.''

She straightened her back in challenge. "Is it also a requirement that she be a virgin?''

"That was uncalled-for.''

"Just like this conversation. It's none of your business what painting I buy or whom I choose for a lover. I didn't ask for your opinion. I'm going to buy that painting now—" she pointed toward it "—for my living room, without any grief from you."

"Fine," he snapped.

"Good."

"You won't hear another word from me." He folded his arms across his chest and glared at her.

"Terrific." She glared right back at him.

"Not another word."

"Just dandy. Start anytime."

"Fine." He clamped his lips shut and stared at a point somewhere behind her left shoulder.

Clay kept his promise. He didn't speak while Jessica paid for the painting and arranged to have it shipped to Los Angeles. And when they stepped back into the sunshine and began wandering aimlessly down the street, he looked silently ahead.

After an hour of it, the quiet was beginning to drive Jessica crazy. His silence, she decided, was worse than his badgering. She felt as if she might explode with it. Turning her head, she stared at him, willing him to speak. Of course, he didn't oblige her.

She balled her hands into fists of frustration and increased her pace. Once she was ahead of him, she whirled around. "And I'll tell you another thing, Clay Jones." She poked a finger into his chest. "You owe me another dinner. We agreed to agree today—remember?"

"Yeah, I remember." He moved around her, continuing up the street.

Jessica scurried after him, convinced that she was furious and that Clay was the most annoying man ever born. She grabbed his elbow. "I'm not finished with you, buster."

Buster? His eyes crinkled very slightly at the corners.

"Don't you ever call me 'cookie' or 'tempting morsel' again! I won't have it. Is that clear?"

"Gee," Clay drawled. "At the time I thought it was pretty punny."

Jessica's facial muscles slackened for a moment, then a smile began to twitch at the corners of her mouth. She caught her lower lip in her teeth to hold back a laugh. It didn't work. It seemed he was always making her laugh, making her forget she was annoyed.

Several moments later Jessica took a deep, calming breath. "I didn't think of it that way. I thought you were just being a macho jerk."

Clay grinned, slipping his arm through hers. "Hungry yet?"

Jessica looked up at him in surprise. "Unbelievably, yes."

"How do steaks and wine on the beach sound to you?"

"Sounds wonderful. In fact, throw in a salad and it'd be perfect."

He laughed. "Leave it to sensible Jessica to remember roughage."

"Mmm-hmm, and dessert."

"Dessert?" Clay lifted his eyebrows playfully.

"Sure." She cut him an amused glance. "A meal isn't a meal without dessert. Do you disagree?"

He held up his hands in surrender. "No way, princess. No way."

Four

___

Your house?" Jessica asked incredulously. "We're having dinner at your house?"

"Yeah." He took the helmet that was dangling from her right hand. "You never asked *where* we were going to eat."

She arched one eyebrow. "And you never gave any indication that you lived in Laguna Beach."

Clay tossed an amused glance over his shoulder as he unlocked the door. "You're not going to disagree with my choice of restaurant, are you?"

"Certainly not. But I'm not going to help you cook, either."

While Clay opened a bottle of wine Jessica wandered around the house. The first floor consisted of a large, open living area, the second was a sleeping loft. The exposed beams and nubby, natural fabric on the furniture were perfect with the terra-cotta tile floors scattered with native American rugs. There was even a modern potbelly stove in the corner. It was earthy, open and warm and it reminded her of Clay.

"Do you like it?" he asked, handing her a glass of red wine.

"Mmm . . . very much."

"And you haven't even seen the best part. Come with me." He took her free hand in his and led her across the room.

For one brief moment Jessica was sure he meant the bedroom. But as they passed the ladder to the loft, she realized her mistake and willed her pulse to slow, willed her shallow breathing to become deep and even. When that didn't work she told herself she was simply nervous. Fatigued. Hungry. She told herself it certainly wasn't his hand holding hers or his thumb lightly stroking her wrist that was scrambling her pulse and making her catch her breath.

All thoughts of disturbing physical sensations and sleeping lofts were forgotten as she stepped out onto the deck. It ran the length of the house and extended over the beach. Facing her was an endless expanse of water and sky.

"Oh, Clay, it's lovely!" she murmured, crossing to the rail. The setting sun bathed the world in a palette of pastels; the breeze was damp and salty. Jessica breathed deeply, enjoying the air's tang, a smile playing around the edges of her mouth.

Relaxation crept over her limbs the way a cat stalked a mouse—slowly, patiently, with the inevitability of success. Jessica accepted that inevitability and even welcomed it. Minutes passed. Muscles tight with stress loosened, thoughts of clients and campaigns and decisions disappeared with the violet on the horizon.

Clay stood silently next to her, not wanting to break the spell with words. Her fingers were curled around the railing, her face and body fitted to the wind. She was a strong woman—tough and savvy. He remembered his whimsy after their first meeting, remembered wondering if she was like a Tootsie Pop, hard on the outside and soft in the center, and that he had thought himself ridiculous.

Not ridiculous, not whimsical. She was as soft as a woman could be. His eyes crinkled at the corners. Oh, she would fiercely deny it. She would arch an eyebrow, square her shoulders and try to stare him down. But he wouldn't retreat, wouldn't be intimidated; he'd discovered the truth about Jessica Mann.

Reaching out, he trailed a finger along the curve of her jaw. Her skin was soft and smooth and inviting. "Should I start dinner?"

All that was left of the sunset was a colorful glow where the ocean met the sky, and Jessica regretfully turned her eyes to Clay. "Nature's show is over," she murmured, then smiled. "Yes, I'll keep you company."

"But you won't help." He held out his hand for hers, not bothering to hide the laughter in his voice.

Jessica took his hand. His fingers were strong and warm around hers. She followed him into the kitchen. "I may be practical and sensible, but I'm certainly not domesticated." She perched on a stool and watched him season the steak, smiling at the way he drew his eyebrows together in concentration. "Important stuff?" she teased.

"Yeah." He looked sheepish, then added another dash of garlic. "Okay, I'm a little wacko with seasonings, and sometimes I overdo it—" he waved a fork at her "—but in my own defense, I absolutely *never* underseason."

"Well, that's reassuring," Jessica said dryly, refilling her wineglass. "Where did you learn to cook?"

"Fast Food U." He dimpled. "I had three sisters—three adoring, older sisters. They took care of me even after I was in college."

Jessica watched as he loaded his arms with fresh vegetables, then shut the refrigerator with his hip. "You mean they spoiled you."

"Rotten," he said cheerfully, expertly dicing onion. "When they weren't around to cook for me anymore I relied on fast food. Let me tell you, hamburgers, pizza and tacos get pretty boring after a while."

"Not to mention lacking vitamins and fiber and—"

"Taste," he supplied.

"Mmm-hmm." She snitched a wedge of tomato and popped it into her mouth. "Unhealthy garbage."

"Fattening junk."

Their eyes met, and they laughed in unison. "So you taught yourself to cook."

"Yes, and I love it." He pulled a partial loaf of homemade bread from the refrigerator. "Cooking can be extremely creative, you know."

"Is that so?" She arched an eyebrow playfully. "Personally, I find it tedious and time-consuming. The last thing I want to do when I get home from work is slave in the kitchen. If it weren't for Ali, I'd starve."

"The coals should be ready," he said, picking up the platter of meat. "You still willing to keep me company?"

"Oh, sure. I'll even carry your wine." She slid off the stool and followed him out onto the deck. "It's very good, by the way."

"An amusing little Beaujolais—subtly fruity, insistent but never cloying. Not a bad choice for a barbarian, huh?"

Jessica saw his eyes crinkle at the corners, even though he didn't look at her. How could anyone be so easygoing? He'd never taken offense at anything she'd said, no matter how blunt or uncomplimentary. She, on the other hand, had taken offense at everything about him and had made no secret of it.

She rested her chin on her fist and watched him. The steaks hissed sharply as Clay laid them on the hot wire rack. Was she still taking offense at him? Jessica wondered, her mouth beginning to water as the air was filled with the aroma of grilling meat. Not at his touch, she admitted, nor at his kiss. When they weren't arguing, she even enjoyed his company. It was the essence of Clay that she objected to: his bohemian life-style, his casual attitude toward work. He was irreverent, kooky and irresponsible.

And charming. Which was most unfortunate, Jessica thought, tipping back her head to let more of the smooth, red wine slip down her throat. Most unfortunate, because she forgot all his faults when he was charming her. And it seemed he was charming her most of the time.

"Almost ready." Clay wiped his hands on an apron that said Kiss the Cook and smiled at her. "Would you like to eat out here?"

"I'd love it."

Minutes later they were sitting down to a feast. Clay lifted his glass in a toast. "To the absence of junk food."

As their glasses touched it occurred to Jessica that she'd had enough to drink. She wasn't drunk, just delightfully fuzzy. And so relaxed. She stared at her plate and wondered if she had the energy to lift her fork.

"Dig in, Jess."

"Of course. I was just…" Jessica raised her eyes to meet his. They were dancing with humor. "The amusing little Beaujolais packs quite a punch."

He dimpled. "That's why it's amusing."

Jessica laughed and took a bite of her meat. It was perfectly prepared—warm and pink in the center, slightly blackened on the outside. She suddenly realized how hungry she was and began to eat with gusto. The salad was crisp and fresh, the bread tasted faintly of dill and Parmesan cheese. Everything was seasoned perfectly. Before long she was pushing away her plate and sighing with contentment. It had been a long time since she'd enjoyed a meal as much and she said so.

"I'm glad. I told you before; you're too thin."

He refilled her glass before she had a chance to tell him not to. With a shrug, she took a sip. "You sound just like Ali. She nags me, too."

"Someone has to." Clay leaned back until the chair rocked on two legs.

"Nonsense," Jessica said briskly. "I'm an adult, a capable professional. The last thing I need is a keeper."

Clay didn't argue with her. She'd tilted her chin ever so slightly as she spoke, and narrowed her eyes stubbornly. She needed a keeper all right. That or a wife. He grinned at the thought. She worked too hard, pushed herself to the point of exhaustion. He suspected she breathed, ate and slept her career. And from what he'd seen, she loved every minute of it.

She reminded him of himself three years ago, careening down the fast track toward high blood pressure or a stroke. Obsessed with climbing the ladder to the point of forgetting that life was also about laughter, relaxation, enjoyment. For a while he'd loved it, too. Until his body and his brain had said "No more."

In all honesty, Clay had to admit that the fast track was okay for some. There were people who were hard clear to their core, people who throve on making a deal, no matter what they had to do to get it.

But not Jessica. His eyes skimmed over her. She'd scooted down in her seat, propped her feet on another chair and rested her head on the chair back so she could gaze up at the star-sprinkled sky. Her shoes lay abandoned under her chair and a soft smile played at the corners of her mouth as she wiggled her toes with pleasure. Jessica had the soul of a poet, the heart of a romantic and a core of strawberry jam.

He stood and held out his hand. "The beach beckons. Walk with me, Jess?"

The light was behind him; his features were in shadow, and Jessica wished she could see his eyes. Laughing, she fitted her hand to his and let him pull her up.

The sand was warm as it sifted between her toes and to prolong the sensation she curled them into it with each step. They swung their joined hands between them as they walked and Jessica acknowledged the bounce in her step. She felt like a child, carefree and magically alive.

Jessica glanced at him, then back up at the obsidian sky. "Walking along the beach like this reminds me of the trip we took to Hawaii when I was thirteen. I remember it so clearly because we took few vacations as a family, and it was right before Mother left."

She fell silent, and Clay didn't prod her—she would tell him if she wanted him to know more. She was a woman who kept a tight rein on her emotions, but Clay was patient, because he believed that good things were always worth waiting for.

When she finally spoke, it was with the dreamy quality of an adult recalling a cherished childhood moment. "Ali and I were walking hand in hand. The moon was full, the night was warm.... She and I skipped and giggled...."

Jessica's brow furrowed slightly as if something didn't add up. "Mother was with us, but stayed several feet behind. We walked for a long, long time—I was so tired afterward—but I don't remember Mother ever speaking to us or joining in our fun."

"Where was your father?"

She cocked her head, trying to remember. "I'm not sure.... Wait, he stayed in the room. In fact, he spent a lot of time in the room." She laughed suddenly. "He'd probably eaten too much pineapple. Several times I had horrible stomach aches from stuffing myself with fresh fruit."

"Glutton." He lowered his eyes, admiring her willowy figure.

"Mmm, real porkers, Ali and I." They stopped walking and stood staring out at the mercurial water. "Meals in Hawaii were feasts. For every meal the hotel provided buffets. Not ordinary buffets, but table after table laden with different foods. One long table would be covered with fresh fruits, another with breads and pastries, still another with meats."

"Sounds like a veritable smorgas-gorge." Reaching out, he toyed with the wisps of hair at her nape.

"For us, yes. As children we were both...well...round." She caught her breath as Clay began softly stroking her neck.

"There's nothing wrong with enjoying earthy pleasures, Jess." He felt her pulse scramble under his fingers, saw her eyes flutter shut with pleasure. "If food was only to fuel our bodies, it wouldn't taste so good. I enjoy eating...just as I enjoy touching."

He began unbraiding her hair. "If hair wasn't meant to be touched it wouldn't be so soft, so fragrant." He ran his hands through the freed tresses, letting them stream over his fingers like blond silk. "I've wanted to do that for a long time," he murmured, tangling his fingers in the soft mass for one more possessive moment, before letting it tumble to her shoulders.

He cupped her face in his hands and their eyes met. "And skin...would it be as flawless as alabaster...as inviting as cream, if I weren't meant to caress it?"

When he touched her, she wanted more. She'd never known a greed like this, had never wanted so badly that it was a gnawing ache in her belly. He explored her face with his fingertips, brushing, skimming, caressing. His touch was unbelievably gentle. She wasn't deceived—there was nothing tentative about his exploration. It was thorough and decisive. He was absorbing her.

Clay trailed his thumbs over her lips and smiled as he felt the shuddered exhalations against his fingertips. "And lips...would they be as moist and sweet as strawberries at the peak of the season if they weren't meant to be tasted?"

He briefly caught her lower lip in his teeth and teased her tongue with his own. Jessica thought she was going to die of wanting and sagged against him. She found his taste delicious. Heady. Addictive. Opening her mouth she asked for more. Their tongues twined, each drinking in the sweetness of the other. Pressed together they sank to the sand.

"My sweet, sweet, Jessica..." He placed kisses everywhere—her fluttering eyelids, her delicate eyebrows, her fine, straight nose. "How I want you...."

She arched her back as his hands whispered over her breasts, then her mind reeled as his lips followed his hands. The love words he murmured were incredible intoxicants. She'd thought the wine potent, had thought feeling fuzzy and lightheaded delicious. Compared to Clay's lovemaking the wine was impotent, even laughable, and sensations raced over her that made fuzziness and lightheadedness commonplace. She felt absolutely, wickedly alive.

Leaning on an elbow, Clay gazed down at her flushed features. The dullness of the sand was a foil for her shining hair, spread out, circling her head like a Byzantine halo.

This was crazy, insane. He wanted her now, wanted to slip inside her with the surf pounding in his ears, the warm wind stroking his back. As he watched, her eyes fluttered open. They were stormy with passion, but in moments would begin to clear. He wanted her now, with her stormy eyes and flushed cheeks, and she would acquiesce. Later she would be furious...at herself, at him. He didn't want to take her; he wanted her to give herself to him openly, honestly and completely.

He trailed a finger from her brow, across her lips, over her breasts. Clay felt her nipples tighten under his attention and groaned as his arousal became painful. "Jessica...Jessica..." He rested his forehead against hers. "You're driving me crazy."

"Impossible," she whispered, rubbing her nose against his. "You're already crazy."

"You're a hard woman, Jess." Her lips, still moist and softly parted, were too tempting, and he caught them again.

He smiled as he pulled away. "I'm a little eccentric, that's all."

Jessica paled; that was how her father had described Clay. She'd fought him, fought to be treated as an equal, fought to have her opinion as a professional count. And here she was, her mind emptied of everything but cheap wine and an irresponsible man, making love on the beach like a drunken teenager.

Reality came crashing down on her. The hands that moments before had caressed him pushed at his shoulders.

He rolled off her without argument, watching as she jumped up and, with jerky movements, brushed the sand off the seat of her linen slacks. "What's wrong, Jess?"

"Nothing," she snapped, praying that he would let the incident pass. She didn't want to talk about what had happened between them, because she didn't know what to say. Her emotions were at war with her intellect, creating a tangle of conflicting messages and sensations. It unnerved her, and that angered her. She was a woman with direction, a woman whose every step was clearly thought out and was unmistakably the right move. She wasn't accustomed to confusion, and uncertainty was an enigma.

"Oh?" In one fluid movement Clay stood—he didn't bother brushing the sand away—and faced her. "Until a minute ago I thought life threw some pretty great curves, thought what we had going was pretty great. I don't think I'm out of line asking why you're suddenly acting like a spoiled brat."

Jessica swept away the hair the wind blew in her eyes and faced him evenly. "This afternoon I asked you not to kiss me again."

"With words, Jess. Words can lie when eyes—when bodies—cannot." Clay grabbed her hands because he needed to touch her, needed to connect with her physically as he tried to reach her spiritually. Her hands quivered in his, telling him what she refused to say. "Dishonest words mean nothing," he finished, his eyes searching hers.

He was right, damn it. Part of her wanted him to make love to her, make love to her until the intoxication he brought was her only reality. The other part of her, the sane part, knew that sometimes people wanted what wasn't good for them, and that often the want was as overpowering as it was destructive. Lives were irrecoverably altered, even ruined, by giving in to desires and Jessica Mann refused to be a casualty.

She met his gaze, answering his nonverbal questions with confidence. The boardroom Jessica, the Jessica who'd swayed the surliest of clients was back, control flowing over her like a healing balm.

"By its very nature honesty is subjective," she said quietly. "There are many truths for any situation, for any two people. The individual must make a choice about what is true for him or her. My truth, Clay, is that I don't want you to touch or kiss me again."

"And that's it?" He dropped her hands. "No real explanation, just a quasi-philisophical statement about honesty?" He stared out at the water for a moment before speaking again. A muscle jumped in his jaw. "You're good, Jessica. You know just the right buttons to push, the right words to spit out. There's no need to tell you my truth—it's invalid because it's subjective. And if I argue with you, I'm a jerk for not respecting yours."

Suddenly, Jessica couldn't meet his eyes. She felt as if she'd cheated him, made an unfair business deal. She stared at a point over his left shoulder, feeling small and unclean. Those feelings were ridiculous, she scolded herself. She'd done nothing wrong, had only played to win. And she'd been honest—not open—but honest in a roundabout way. Her spine stiffened. "We're colleagues, Clay. I'd like to think we can put aside our personal differences and work together."

Clay made a sound that was a cross between a laugh and a groan. "What you're asking is impossible, Jessica. Smile at me, accidentally brush against me, and I'll want you." By sheer force of will, he made her look at him. "How's that for truth, lady? Too subjective?" When she didn't answer, when she just stared blankly at him, he added curtly, "Forget it. I don't need this, Jess. My life was going smoothly before..." He dragged both hands through his hair in frustration. "Forget it, I'll drive you home."

Without another word, he spun on his heels and headed down the beach toward his house. His eyebrows lowered in thought. Why didn't he just leave her alone? Jessica represented everything he'd left behind three years ago. The obsession. The workaholism. The single-minded pursuit of success. Her life-style had caught him once before; could it again? Could his fascination with Jessica suck him back into that self-destructive race? He, of all people, knew the seductive pull of power, of being the best. He'd been trapped before.

No. Clay's jaw tightened in determination. Never again. If it came to a choice between Jessica and his freedom, he would tell her goodbye.

Jessica followed Clay slowly. There was a tightness in her chest; it was a heavy, aching knot. Between that and her racing heart, it was difficult to breathe. She wrapped her arms around herself. Why did he have to be so open, so uncomplicated? He lived by the old adage: "If it feels good, do it." He didn't plot, didn't plan, didn't agonize; Clay Jones attacked, jumped in with both feet and didn't look back. His attitude toward work, his very life-style attested to that fact.

She couldn't live that way and was furious with him for asking her to, even if it was just for an evening, just for an interlude, and she was furious with him for confusing her, for making her both question and feel guilty about her choices. That was why her heart was racing and her muscles were heavy. No wonder she couldn't catch her breath—adrenaline was racing through her, her blood pressure was surely skyrocketing.

Clay was waiting for her on the deck, his expression tight and unreadable. Jessica silently climbed the stairs, stewing over her position, using the time to decide how to handle this awkward and unfamiliar situation. *How do you handle a man whom you've been passionately embracing only moments before?* Jessica wondered. Passionately embracing? She almost groaned out loud. That sounded so sane, so civilized, like a description of a chaste love scene from a forties movie. What she'd experienced with Clay had been erotic oblivion. Color crept up her cheeks; she knew it and ignored it.

She would handle Clay, his insanity and his silence, the same way she handled a client who wanted tasteless advertising—with impeccable class and unflappable cool.

"Monday," she said as she reached the deck, "I'm calling Ty and Sandra Miller to make an appointment for Tuesday or Wednesday morning."

"Fine." He locked the sliding glass doors behind them.

"Don't forget to include suggestions for the store interiors with the rest of your designs." She hurried after him. "Tell me now if you're going to have a problem meeting that deadline."

She drew her eyebrows together when he just shrugged and handed her a motorcycle helmet. "I'm taking your silence as the sign to go ahead. I'll notify you of the day and time." Clay's only response was to kick-start the bike. The noise was deafening, and Jessica expelled a sigh of relief, grateful that she wouldn't have to make inane conversation or bear awkward silence all the way back to L.A. She swung her leg over the seat and wrapped her arms around Clay's middle.

The distance of twenty-four hours hadn't dimmed the memory of her fight with Clay, or lessened the turbulent emotions that fight provoked. Jessica tossed and turned, glared at the clock, cursed the time with the fluency of a cabbie caught in a traffic jam, then gave up. It was futile to lie in bed, her mind racing, and pretend that sleep was imminent. Maybe a peanut butter sandwich and a glass of milk would help, she thought, slipping out of bed and heading to the kitchen.

The light over the sink was on; Ali was still out. Jessica smiled. Her sister kept late hours and a string of "only-friends" men at her beck and call. She and Ali were nothing alike, and it never ceased to amaze her, especially considering their childhood circumstances, that they were so close. But Ali hadn't given up—she'd been determined that they would be friends and had won her over.

Jessica shook her head as she heard the key in the lock. *Thank God,* she thought, acknowledging relief. Her life would be a lot grayer without her wacky sister.

"Ali," she called out. "I'm in the kitchen. You can stop tiptoeing." Jessica slathered peanut butter on a piece of Ali's homemade wheat bread, looked longingly at the grape jelly—she knew she couldn't do that to her body tonight—then poured a glass of milk.

"Hi, Sissy," Ali said, flouncing into the kitchen. "Pour me a glass, will you?" She rummaged in the cookie jar and pulled out a sandwich cookie, paused for a moment, then dived in for another. "Couldn't sleep, huh?"

Jessica's expression was amused as she rested her chin on her fist and watched her sister. Ali's hair, a golden-brown mane of layered waves, was wind-tossed into funky disarray. She wore a brilliantly colored silk dress with spaghetti straps and handkerchief hem; her legs were tan, her feet bare.

Jessica lifted an eyebrow. "Where were you, and what happened to your shoes?"

"Dancing at the Hard Rock." Ali dunked her cookie in the milk, took a bite, then rolled her eyes with pleasure. "I took my shoes off and couldn't find them again. They were my favorites, too.... Damn."

"Who'd you go with, Bob or Jake?"

"Neither." Ali plopped onto the stool next to Jessica and hooked her right foot around the bottom rung. "They were both getting too possessive, so I went with Ted."

"The tall, serious-looking guy?" Jessica asked, chasing a crumb around her plate with her index finger.

"Not serious, moody. He's a writer, you know. We drank Mimosas all night."

"Orange juice and champagne," Jessica murmured absently, a small frown forming between her eyebrows.

"Mmm-hmm, yummy." Ali shot her a questioning and concerned look. "What's wrong, Jessica? This is the third time in the last couple of weeks you've been unable to sleep, and those are only the times I've caught you. I'm starting to worry. What was it this time: a new client, a fight with Daddy, a presentation?"

Jessica frowned and rubbed her temples. Her insomnia, although she would deny it to everyone but herself, was beginning to worry her. "You're nagging again, and there have only been three times." She took a bite of her sandwich, her expression thoughtful. "Believe it or not, I was thinking about Mother."

"Mother? What brought this on?" Ali asked, reaching for her second cookie.

Jessica shrugged. "Clay and I took a walk on the beach last night, and it brought back memories of our trip to Hawaii." Ignoring Ali's raised eyebrows at the mention of a moonlight stroll with Clay, she finished her milk and rinsed her glass. After a moment, Jessica glanced over her shoulder and smiled. "Do you remember what she used to call me?"

"Sure. She called you Jess."

"Funny, until Clay nobody but Mother called me that."
She turned back to the window, her eyes filled with unexpected and unwanted tears. "She used to sing to us."

"Yeah, and make up those silly bedtime stories."

"And now," they said in unison, mimicking their mother,
"it's time for the Jess and Ali show."

After their laughter abated, Ali touched Jessica's shoulder. "It was never the same without you; her heart was broken because you'd chosen him."

Jessica's expression tightened. "She left us."

"She left Daddy," Ali corrected. "Her life with him was an impossible purgatory. Surely you can see that."

Was it that bad for her? Jessica wondered, lowering her eyes. Had she only seen and felt what she'd wanted to? At thirteen she'd given her father total allegiance, and until now, had never looked back. Thirteen was a vulnerable, uncertain age; she'd been furious that her mother had left, hurt clear to her gut, and terrified about the future. And she'd directed all that ugly, adolescent emotion at her mother.

"You should call her," Ali said. "She loves you."

The tears were back, filling her eyes, blurring her vision; Jessica tried to blink them away and her eyes burned from the effort. "It's been years," she said softly. "I'll have to think about it."

"You're still her little girl, Jessica." Ali's eyes were as wet as her sister's. "She mourns for you."

Tears slipped down Jessica's cheeks, and she brushed them away. She took a deep breath; her chest and head ached with the need to sob. "I'll think about it, Ali, I promise," she said, her voice husky with tears.

Five

Jessica stood waiting at her office door. Clay saw her tap her foot and check her watch, but he didn't hurry; he liked looking at her. She was wearing a navy-blue linen suit and a red and navy bow tie, nestled in front of the collar of her white blouse. She looked crisp, capable and professional. A month ago he'd allowed her uniform, her armor, to fool him; he'd thought this woman, with all her poetry and fire, a barracuda. His grin turned into a smile. He'd thought her a cold fish, when in actuality she was as alive as the ocean, as inviting as the sun.

He should still be furious about the other night, but he wasn't. He'd resolved over the weekend to cut his losses and forget her, and here he was gazing at her like a lovesick schoolboy. Wondering at the warmth unfurling inside him, he crossed the room.

Jessica checked her watch for the third time and swore under her breath. Where was he? If he missed this meeting he was off the account—Jessica's stomach fluttered at the thought—no matter what her father said. Damn it, where was he? She took a deep breath and silently groaned; she hadn't slept the night before, her palms were sweating, her chest was tight. Stage fright—she got it before every presentation, before every meeting with a new client. These jitters were a constant source of irritation because she didn't understand them. The minute she held out her hand and introduced herself it would be all over, she would be in perfect control—it infuriated her that she had to suffer until then.

"Good morning, Jess. Ready?" God, she smelled good, Clay thought, wanting to move closer but knowing she would feel pressured. He inhaled; the scent was floral without being sweet, spicy without being aggressive. It reminded him of her.

Jessica turned, her eyes raking over him with a greediness that shocked her, that drove all thoughts of nerves and presentations from her mind. It was only a moment, but in that moment she absorbed everything about him—the expression in his eyes, the fact that he'd gotten some sun over the weekend, that he was relaxed and confident. As the last observation registered, her anxiety returned. "You're here, thank goodness. Now we can get going."

Clay's eyes skimmed over her, taking in her tenseness and the faint blue circles under her eyes. "Is something wrong?"

"No, of course not. I'm fine. Let's go." She grabbed her portfolio and headed toward the elevator. It was empty and Jessica used the opportunity to sag against the back wall and take a deep breath.

Clay followed without comment, his expression concerned. "If you're ill, we can reschedule—"

"Don't be ridiculous," she said, straightening and staring at the floor number indicator. She felt his steady gaze and gave in. "Oh, all right. I get stage fright before presentations, that's all. I've tried to control it and can't. Don't you dare feel sorry for me."

They stepped off the elevator into the parking garage. The concrete structure was damp and smelled of exhaust. "Give me the keys," Clay said, holding out his hand, palm up. When her eyes heated, he added, "I don't doubt your ability to drive. I just thought you might like to relax."

"Thank you," Jessica said, handing him the keys.

Minutes later Clay was pulling into traffic. When he was safely in his lane, he shot her a sympathetic glance. "Feel better?"

"No." Her fingers curled into her palms, she swore and relaxed them. "Actually, I feel like a jerk. I'm an adult, a capable professional—these panic attacks are ridiculous."

"Don't be so hard on yourself, Jessica. Seasoned performers get stage fright, the best students work themselves into a frenzy before a test. Relax, use all the adrenaline to your advantage."

"If my father could see me now he'd call me a hysterical female." Jessica lowered her eyes. "That, or a dizzy blonde." After a moment of silence, she continued. "You see, he never believed I could make it in advertising."

"Because you're a woman."

"Yes. I suspect he still thinks I'll trip up."

Clay covered her clenched hands with one of his own. "If your father would call being human 'tripping up' then he's more machine than man. Have your nerves ever affected your performance?"

"No, of course not." A ghost of a smile flickered across her face as she realized her palms had stopped sweating. "You're being very sweet."

"Yeah, I'm sweet, I'm loveable, I'd make a good pet. Wanna take me home, lady?" He shot her a puppy-dog look.

A deliciously erotic picture shot into her head and Jessica blushed and lowered her gaze. "Keep your eyes on the road, Clay. I want to make it to this presentation in one piece."

They made it to the presentation, but considering the turn of events, Jessica almost wished they hadn't. When the pencil she was holding snapped in two Jessica quietly slipped the splintered pieces into her jacket pocket. Of course they didn't notice, she thought, her eyes narrowing on the presentation in progress. Clay was doing everything but tap-dance for them.

Absently she trailed her finger along the edge of the teakwood conference room table; her furious eyes never left Clay. He was determined to beat her and was going to great lengths to do so. A good presentation usually consisted of a half dozen sample designs so the client could get an idea of the look of the campaign, and a written proposal that included a creative rationale and marketing plan. That was what she provided.

But Clay, the rat, had done twice that. He'd included a dozen designs, a television storyboard and sample radio spots. He'd also gone as far as to cite ten previous, conceptually similar campaigns for bakery products and note their success.

He wasn't playing fair, Jessica fumed, listening as Clay concluded his presentation; she couldn't cite any similar campaigns, because she was breaking new ground. Her eyes narrowed with thought, then the edges of her mouth tilted in a smile—she wasn't out of the running yet.

"Thank you, Clay." Jessica smiled coolly, nodding in his direction as she stood and faced Sandra and Ty Miller. "We're offering you two very different directions to choose from. One is proven but traditional, the other is unproven, but fresh, innovative. Both will increase your sales, so it's now a question of what look you want. We're talking about image—your advertising should reflect you, your company, your product. When a campaign is successful, as ours will be, the buyers will picture your commercial in their heads, hum your music, immediately recognize your logo.

Good advertising design and its product become inextricably bound to one another.

"Consider the surreal, erotic fantasies for Channel No. Five; they're unmistakable as well as compelling. But, more importantly, the consumer links the fragrance with the world that the commercials portray. 7-Up's seventies tag line The Uncola convinced a whole generation that it was light and clean, a different, therefore better choice. And who wouldn't instantly place a rainbow-colored apple? The Apple Corporation wanted to persuade the public that their products were the easiest and most fun to use, and their colorful, playful graphics did so." Jessica slanted Clay a triumphant glance before continuing. "Again, it comes down to how you want the public to perceive you and your product, in this case, as homespun or high tech."

"Thank you both," Sandra Miller said, beaming at Jessica. "Both presentations were excellent, but in my opinion there's only one choice."

"My sentiments exactly," her brother added, shooting a smile across the table at Clay.

Jessica held her breath and tried to appear relaxed. Her palms were sweating again and her heart was thumping furiously in her chest. This was her chance to prove to her father that she could do it all, the creative and the business sides. Jessica slowly exhaled as Sandra began to speak.

"Jessica, I'm confident I also speak for my brother when I say how excited I am about your approach to Cookies from Heaven's advertising. I'm tired of clone advertising, most of which is either tasteless, boring or both. The contemporary graphics, music and interiors you suggested in your presentation are exactly what I want."

Jessica relaxed as her heart slowed its frenetic pace. *Thank God,* she thought. *Thank God—*

"Sandra, you must be kidding!" Ty Miller faced his sister in astonishment. "That stuff is great in an art gallery or in between songs on MTV, but keep in mind, Sandra, that we're selling cookies . . . not designer clothing.''

Jessica's heart sank, but she gave no indication of it when she spoke. ''You might think your product is just a cookie, but I guarantee you, the public thinks of you as a luxury. At a dollar twenty-five each, your cookies are a designer label. Calvin Klein has to convince the public that his jeans are *worth* twice what others cost, and we have to do the same thing. The better, the more unusual, the more current we look, the more convincing we'll be.''

''Jessica's right,'' Clay inserted smoothly. ''We have to look good, professional and slick, but that doesn't necessarily mean high tech. The traditional approach to selling cookies is a proven winner. It works because none of us can escape our childhood memories.'' He grinned as Jessica shot him a withering look.

''I agree with Clay.'' Ty faced his sister. ''When I think of cookies, I think of Mom and her apron, baking goodies on Saturday.''

''You would,'' Sandra said, glaring at her brother, ''because you're not a woman. I refuse to promote all the sexist garbage that anchors women to the stove. And I'm sick and tired of advertising fostering the idea that only Mom can cook. Let's face facts. Just as there is no Mrs. Paul making fish sticks, there is no Mrs. making Cookies from Heaven.''

''Oh, grow up, Sandra.'' Ty ran a hand through his hair in disgust. ''Don't use our company as a vehicle for all that feminist—''

''Don't you dare say what I think you're going to, brother dear, or I'll be forced to call you what you are.''

''What's that?'' Ty's tone was dry. ''A chauvinist pig? A sexist jerk?''

Jessica silently groaned and glanced at Clay. She couldn't believe it—he looked amused! He was leaning back in his chair, his arms were folded across his chest and a smile twitched at the corners of his mouth. How could he find this situation funny? They were here to sell their ideas and instead had initiated a family feud. The brother and sister were tossing insults at each other with the speed and fury of adolescent boys participating in a cafeteria food fight, and worse, there was no sign of it stopping anytime soon.

Jessica held a hand to her forehead and winced as Ty called Sandra a selfish twit. Then Sandra shot back that he had the intelligence and sensitivity of a Cro-Magnon man. Her stomach tightened. There had to be a way to make peace. They should either do that, or sneak out without being noticed. Deciding that being forceful was the only answer, Jessica stood, cleared her throat and took a deep breath. "Excuse me!"

Thirty minutes later, Jessica slumped into the Volvo's front passenger seat and rubbed her temples. "What a fiasco! Tell me this has just been a bad dream, Clay. Tell me this morning was somebody's idea of a twisted joke."

"Lighten up, Jess." Clay slipped into traffic. "At least we got a reaction."

"Great," Jessica muttered in disgust. "Tell that to my father when he asks when we're going into production. We don't make a cent until we do, so naturally he's anxious for us to get started."

Clay slammed on the brakes as a car cut in front of him. He gestured rudely at the other driver before glancing back at Jessica. "It's not unusual for a client to spend several weeks mulling over the presentation before giving the final okay."

"That's not the point," Jessica said, frowning. "I wanted this to go through quickly and smoothly."

"You mean you wanted to impress your father."

She looked away. When she spoke her tone was low but fierce. "It's important that he have complete confidence in me. At seventeen I promised myself that he'd take back his doubt, that he would apologize for not believing in me."

Clay covered her clenched hands with one of his own. How could he tell her that her father would never admit to being wrong? How could he tell her that, in all probability, her father didn't even consider that he'd treated her unfairly in the first place?

Clay glanced at her determined expression and sighed. It was dangerous to look for satisfaction from other people; they would let you down again and again. Real happiness could only come from within, and once it did, no one could take it away from you. But he couldn't tell her those things—she wasn't ready to hear them.

He squeezed her hand lightly. "How about lunch?"

"Lunch? How can you think about food?" Jessica twisted in her seat to stare at him.

"Because I'm hungry," Clay said simply. "And I bet you didn't have breakfast. You'll feel better after you eat."

Jessica groaned. "I won't feel better if I eat, I'll throw up. My stomach's in knots, my head's throbbing and my heart's a hammer in my chest."

"Jessica, you've got to learn to relax." Clay's tone was serious and concerned. "You can't stress your body like this day after day and not expect retaliation. I'm worried about you."

Jessica blinked as unexpected tears filled her eyes. *Ridiculous,* she scolded herself, she was definitely not the "tears" type. Clay seemed to bring out the worst in her—seesaw emotions, unprofessional behavior, confusion. And now anger. "Perhaps you don't realize how serious this situation is."

"Whatever you say, Jess. If you're sure you don't want lunch, I'm going to stop at the Happy Burger drive-thru, okay?"

Jessica drew in an angry breath. "I don't believe you! We have a potential disaster on our hands, and all you can think about is your stomach. It was bad enough when *we* were fighting over which direction to use. Now the clients are fighting. How do you propose we sway these two stubborn and volatile people? And, putting all that aside, do you realize how close we came to losing our credibility? We behaved unprofessionally, it's as simple as that."

"How can you say that, Jessica? We delivered two spectacular presentations." Clay pulled into the drive-thru line.

"That's another thing—" Jessica bit back her words as Clay began ordering into a microphone located in a giant clown's belly. When he'd finished, she continued. "Don't you think you went a little overboard this morning? You were determined to beat me and did twice the required work to do so."

Clay handed the food to Jessica. "Don't project your ambitions onto me. You're the one who's so determined to win. You're also the one who's out to prove something, the one who turned this into a contest—not me. I wasn't trying to beat you, Jessica. All I wanted to do was present my ideas to the best of my ability."

Jessica shot him a furious glance. "Oh, please. Are you telling me you always provide twelve sample designs, storyboards, radio spots and an advertising history?" Her tone was incredulous. "That would be extreme even for an overachiever."

Clay's jaw tightened. "Meaning what? That I'm too lazy to do that much work? Perhaps you expected a bum like me to give a slipshod presentation? Has it ever crossed your mind that I enjoy what I do, that perhaps the industry's standards aren't high enough for me?"

"I didn't say that, Clay. I only meant..." Her words trailed off. What did she mean? Had she once, just once, considered that his presentation had been terrific because he was a terrific creative director? Heat crept into her cheeks at the answer, and she looked uncomfortably out the window.

After several moments of silence, Jessica glanced back at him. "I'm sorry, Clay," she said, her tone full of regret.

"When Father hired me away from Ad House, I thought finally, finally I'd proven myself to him. And when he gave me this account—a big, important account—I was sure he was confident of my ability."

"Enter the wandering creative director," Clay said softly.

"Yes." Jessica alternately plucked at, then smoothed the cuff of her blouse. "You see, Father put me in charge of this account, but took my control away by not allowing me to choose the creative director."

"He gave you a toy, then told you not to play with it," Clay murmured sympathetically.

"Mmm." Jessica reached into the bag for a French fry. "When you missed the initial meeting with Ty and Sandra, I was sure I'd been right about what I perceived to be your attitude problem."

"My tardiness was completely unintentional, I assure you." Clay unwrapped a burger. "A flight that should have taken three hours took six. We sat for three hours in Houston, of all places, with engine trouble. The airline wouldn't let anyone off the plane, or I would have called."

"Why didn't you tell me that right away?" Jessica asked in astonishment.

Clay shrugged and took a bite of his burger. "I've never liked people who made excuses. I missed the meeting. There was nothing that could be done to alter that fact." He shot her a quick grin. "Besides, would any explanation have changed your opinion of me?"

A reluctant smile tugged at the edges of her mouth as she fished around in the bag for another French fry. "I'm not going to answer that question, Clay."

Clay laughed and reached for another burger. "Sure you don't want a hamburger?" he asked. "They have extra cheese and onions."

"God, no." Jessica tapped a finger against her cheek. "We've got a big problem, Clay."

"Bigger than onion breath, Jess?"

She choked back a laugh. She had no business being amused. "I suspect neither of the headstrong Millers is going to change their mind, which means we have to come up with another creative direction, and pronto."

Clay turned into the parking garage and started up the ramp. "Let's give them a few days to fight it out. You never know, one of them might weaken." He slipped into one of the spots reserved for The Mann Agency.

"I doubt it," Jessica said gloomily, unfastening her seat belt and opening the car door. "We never should have presented two ideas. We've confused them, and in the process tripled our work. It was our job as professionals to decide on one direction and sell the client on it."

"We screwed up, Jess." He linked his arm with hers as they walked to the elevator. "What do you suggest?"

Jessica groaned and pressed the button for the thirtieth floor. "We're going to have to come up with something great, something better than what we presented today, but at the same time combine elements of what they both liked."

"That's a tall order." Clay paused, glancing up at the floor numbers as they were illuminated in the indicator. After a moment, he met her eyes. "It's going to call for lots of after-hours' work. Why don't we start tonight, over dinner?"

Jessica caught her breath as he lowered his gaze to her mouth. Her pulse fluttered at the need in his eyes. She wanted him, wanted to lean against him and give him her lips, offer him her need. She looked away. Wanting him the way she did was insane, and she wasn't a woman suited to insanity. The intoxication he promised was alluring, but she liked both feet planted firmly on the ground.

"The only after hours we'll be spending together," she replied coolly, "will be in the office. We're colleagues, Clay, nothing more." The doors slid open, and Jessica stepped into the reception area. "I'll consult my calendar and let you know when I'm available."

Without warning, Clay grabbed her elbow and swung her around. His eyes flashed angrily, a muscle twitched in his jaw and Jessica took a deep, steadying breath.

"You're such a hypocrite, Jessica. Why don't you admit what you're feeling?"

"All right," Jessica said icily. "I'm furious. Now excuse me."

"I don't think so." He lowered his voice. "I think you're afraid because I make you feel."

Her eyes narrowed. "This is neither the time nor the place to discuss my feelings, Clay. Let go of my arm."

"When you look at me," he murmured, his voice husky, "your eyes turn to fire. And when I touch you—" he moved closer "—you tell me with those sultry eyes that you don't want me stop."

Clay loosened his grip, then began rhythmically stroking her arm. Jessica drew a labored breath. Her comfortable linen suit suddenly felt like hot, heavy swaddling clothes, and she longed to be free of it. But no fabric could be as hot, as binding as his eyes: they drilled into her, holding her captive, demanding honesty.

"Have dinner with me, Jess. Let's talk about this incredible thing between us." Their bodies almost brushed, her fluttering breath was warm against his cheek. "Just dinner, Jessica."

"I don't know." Confused, Jessica shifted her gaze to a point over his left shoulder; it was a moment before she realized that her eyes had met her father's. His expression was shocked, and she froze as the picture she and Clay must make—bodies almost touching, eyes tangling, cheeks flushed—shot into her head.

"My God!" Jessica whispered, horrified at her own behavior, mortified that her father had witnessed it. When she looked up again, her father was gone. Stepping away from Clay, she squared her shoulders and lifted her chin.

Clay knew he'd lost her. He'd seen the cold creep into her eyes, had felt her arm stiffen under his hand. "Don't do this, Jessica. Have dinner with me, let's talk."

"I'm sorry, Clay." Her fingers trembled slightly as she straightened her jacket. "I have a lot of work to do. Excuse me."

Welcome to prison, Jessica thought sourly, hanging her jacket on the coat tree and tossing her briefcase onto her desk. She wandered to the window and stared longingly out at the blue and gold morning. The only sun she would feel today was the sun that warmed the glass, and the only breeze she would feel was the one kicked up by the fan used to dry type in the art department.

Jessica frowned; why should that bother her? This office was the physical proof of her achievement; all she had to do was look around her to know the satisfaction of having built something through hard work and dedication.

Boring. Jessica pushed that word out of her mind. That simply wasn't true, she assured herself. She loved her career. It was challenging, fulfilling.... What else did she need in her life? Nothing. Jessica turned away from the window and walked determinedly to her desk. She certainly didn't need a blonde barbarian with a wicked smile and teasing eyes.

She was distracted, that was all. Concerned over the cookie account, frustrated at her father's attitude. So what if Clay hadn't touched her in—Jessica checked her watch—two days and twenty-two hours? Groaning, she slouched in her chair, then straightened because she never slouched. She needed coffee, she was coming down with something, having a nervous breakdown. Hoping coffee really was the answer, Jessica buzzed Barbara.

By noon she was sure it wasn't coffee she needed. She'd had six cups, and since she'd survived all that caffeine she was as healthy as a horse and definitely not having a nervous breakdown. But the cookie account, now *that* was a different matter. Jessica slipped off her reading glasses, then thoughtfully tapped them against her desk.

"Hope you like pepperoni."

Jessica lifted her eyes, and smiled with pleasure. "Clay." Her voice was husky, and she cleared her throat. "What? No, I—"

"Good." Clay placed the flat, square box in a clear space on her desk. He opened it with a flourish. "Pepperoni, onions and extra cheese."

A moment ago food had been the farthest thing from her mind. Now she was famished. In fact, she couldn't remember anything having ever looked as delicious as that pizza did right now. Stomach growling, she reached for a piece of the pie.

After several minutes and two slices of pizza, she asked, "What brought this on?"

"Rumor has it you visited the coffeepot six times. I knew you wouldn't stop for lunch, so I took matters into my own hands."

Jessica swallowed convulsively. "Still think I'm too thin, do you?"

Clay's eyes swept tenderly over her. "No, I think you need someone to take care of you."

"Oh." She wasn't sure if she was offended or touched. A month ago she would have been furious. And she should be—after all, she could take care of herself—but there was a warm, tingling sensation creeping over her, as if she'd drunk too much champagne, and it made her feel too good to be furious.

The truth was, she didn't know how to handle this situation. Jessica began systematically shredding her napkin. Warm, tingling sensations were definitely not her forte. No, she preferred icy calm and stodgy old geezers.

Clay lowered his eyes to her fidgeting fingers. "Have you talked to either of the feuding Millers?"

Jessica's head snapped up. She followed his gaze to her hands, and heat tinted her cheeks. She swept the shreds of paper into her hand and dumped them into the trash. "Yes, I talked to Sandra this morning. No luck."

"Got any ideas?"

"I'd hoped you would have some," Jessica said glumly. "I keep drawing a blank. What's next?"

"Today's Wednesday. Let's give them until Friday." He dropped his empty soda can into the garbage, then stood. "If they haven't come to an agreement by then, we'll call an agency creative meeting for Monday morning. Ten heads are better than one." He paused at the door. "Enjoyed lunch, Jess."

She stared at the now-empty doorway. He hadn't touched her, yet she felt suddenly bereft of warmth; he hadn't said much, yet the office now seemed quiet and far too isolated. Sighing, Jessica turned her gaze away from the door and picked up her glasses.

Jessica dropped her keys back into her purse. She was bone weary, her head was pounding, her spirits were at an all-time low. She and her father had had another argument and—she checked her watch—it'd been two days and seven hours since she'd spoken to Clay.

Jessica scowled, kicked off her shoes and tossed her purse onto the couch. Her mood had nothing to do with Clay, or with the fact that her weekend stretched before her with nothing more exciting planned than catching up on the trade journals. Which was fine. She liked quiet weekends.

She was frustrated because today had come and gone with no good news from Cookies from Heaven, and she'd had to call a Monday morning creative meeting. That was what had started the argument with her father.

"Ali," she called out, "I'm home." There was no response, and hearing muffled sounds from the kitchen, she headed that way. *Ali's not alone,* Jessica realized with a smile. The incorrigible flirt. Which poor, lovesick guy was it this time?

Jessica stepped into the kitchen, a smile forming on her lips. The smile faded. The poor, lovesick guy was Clay. Their heads were together as they bent over the oven. And they were laughing. When Clay playfully nudged Ali with his hip, Jessica knew an ache that hurt clear to her soul.

She'd never been jealous of her sister, had never begrudged her any of her male friends, nor had she ever felt inadequate when compared with Ali. Until now.

She curled her fingers into her palms. She didn't want Clay, so why should she care if he'd come to see Ali? Because he'd held her in his arms and made her forget everything but him, she thought quickly. Because he'd touched her in ways she'd never been touched before, and she couldn't stand the thought of him making another woman feel those things.

Because she was crazy about him. She caught her breath at the admission. A heavy, trapped feeling settled in her chest. She didn't need this insane attraction, not when her career was at such a critical point. This was her time, her big break. In a year she would be a nationally recognized name in advertising. An affair with Clay would be time-consuming and impractical and she didn't want him.

But she did. She wanted him with a ferocity she'd never experienced before. She felt timid and bold at the same time, and her first instinct was to run away, to run away and hide from Clay and from her emotions. But she also wanted to strut into the kitchen, slap her sister silly, then haul Clay to the floor and make love to him with the same ferocity that had her reeling just thinking about it.

Clay and Ali exclaimed in unison as they pulled a perfect cheese soufflé from the oven. It was high and golden brown. Jessica's stomach flip-flopped as Clay and Ali's eyes met, as they exchanged knowing glances.

They look good together, Jessica acknowledged, taking a step backward. They're a perfectly matched couple. The truth of that made her lightheaded. They would make beautiful babies, she thought and she flattened her hand on her stomach as a wave of nausea overtook her. Timidity won, and she turned to leave the kitchen.

Clay saw her before she escaped. Her heart sank. "Jess," he said simply.

"Hi, Sissy." Ali carefully set the soufflé on the counter, then tossed the oven mitts into the drawer. "I didn't hear you come in."

"I called out." Jessica folded her arms across her chest and wished she were anywhere but in this kitchen. "You were preoccupied." She stressed the last word, sounding petulant even to her own ears.

"Mmm, and doesn't it look yummy? Clay and I decided to put our chef's hats on." She rubbed her hands together. "The salad's already tossed, the soufflé needs to cool for thirty minutes, and I need a shower. I'm sure you two can amuse yourselves. Ta-ta..." Ali wiggled her fingers and disappeared.

Jessica's gaze wandered from the now-empty doorway to Clay. His hips rested against the counter and his arms were folded. Their eyes met.

"Okay, Jess, what was that crack supposed to mean?"

She raised her eyebrows haughtily. "I'm sure I don't know what you mean."

"'Preoccupied?' Come on, Jess, that was nasty."

"Look, I'm tired, I have a headache, it's been a long day. I don't need this." She spun around and stalked out of the kitchen.

Clay followed her. "Hey!" He caught her hands. "What don't you need, Jessica? What's wrong?"

Jessica slipped her hands from his and lifted her chin defiantly. "Leave me alone, Clay."

His gaze lingered on her stricken face, noting her pale cheeks, and smudges under her eyes. "It's almost eight o'clock. Where've you been?"

"Where do you think? I've been at the office, trying to figure a way out of our predicament." She rubbed the back of her neck while she spoke. "Unlike you, I haven't the time to play around."

Clay's eyes drew together. "Excuse me. Did I miss something?"

He was the picture of confused innocence, which made her all the more angry. She turned on him. "If you want to see Ali, that's fine. In fact, you can come over every night if you like. Just let me know so I can stay away."

Now he understood—she was angry because she was jealous. A soft smile touched his lips, and he took a step toward her. "I didn't stop by to see Ali."

"Oh?" Jessica held her ground even though her instinct told her to run, even though adrenaline was pumping through her, preparing her for flight.

"No." He caught her hands, his voice deepened. "I came for you, Jess."

Her pulse fluttered as Clay traced slow circles on the underside of her wrist. She could imagine the tender, translucent flesh throbbing with her increased heartbeat. She moistened her lips, denial on the tip of her tongue.

"I want you, Jess." He caught her damp lower lip between his teeth and tugged gently. "I can't sleep for wanting you," he murmured as he traced the delicate shape of her ear with his tongue. "I can't stay away.... I can't not push." He trailed his lips down her throat.

Jessica moaned. She felt as if he were devouring her. Every part of her body screamed for his touch, every nerve focused on the spot he was touching. With his touch came a desperate hunger for more. She'd heard of needing, of wanting so much that it hurt, but hadn't believed it could be true. Until now. She hurt, she burned. Whimpering, she offered him her mouth.

Clay tightened his arms around her, his mouth a breath away but not touching hers. "Tell me you want me, Jess. Tell me you need me to make love to you."

She opened her eyes and gazed into his. They were dark with awareness, slightly narrowed with determination. Couldn't he tell? Couldn't he feel the need emanating from her like heat off a window? She moved against him, telling him without words what she wanted.

He rested his forehead against hers. "For some men that would be good enough. But I need more. I need honesty and vulnerability. I need you to give and share all of yourself even though you're afraid."

Her chest tightened, her palms grew damp. He was right; she *was* afraid. He was asking her to toss away the sensible, practical Jessica she'd always known and trusted. He was asking her to strip away her armor and trust only him. Could she do it?

"Look at you two! I leave you alone for five minutes and look what happens!" Ali placed her fists on her hips and grinned at her sister.

Jessica stepped away from Clay, relief washing over her. "We were...um, discussing..." Her cheeks flushed and with trembling fingers she brushed imaginary lint from the sleeve of her jacket.

"And it looked like such a serious discussion." Ali laughed as she swept into the room.

Clay dragged a hand through his hair and cut Ali a frustrated glanced as she passed. "Great timing, Ali," he muttered and was rewarded with her giggle.

"Well, you won't have to worry about me much longer," she said, opening the bottom desk drawer and revealing a foil-wrapped box of chocolates.

Jessica's eyes narrowed and flicked over her sister. "First of all, you just made a major tactical error in showing me that hiding place. Secondly, aren't you a little overdressed, even for a cheese soufflé?''

''Afraid I have to pass on the eggs; Jake's persuaded me to go to Vegas for the weekend.'' Ali frowned and tucked the box back into the drawer. ''He wore me down; you know how I love to gamble.'' A horn sounded from outside. ''That's him, gotta go.'' She paused at the doorway, tossing a menacing look over her shoulder. ''Eat my chocolates and die, Jessica.''

After several moments of silence Jessica looked at Clay. His eyes were filled with laughter.

''Is she always like that?'' he asked with a small shake of his head.

''If you mean, always overwhelmingly energetic, pathologically charming—yes.'' Jessica rubbed the back of her neck. ''Be careful. Stronger men than you have fallen.''

''I thought we'd been through that already.'' He watched her roll her shoulders in discomfort. She looked exhausted. ''Turn around.'' When she complied, he began gently massaging her shoulders and neck. ''No wonder you have a headache; your muscles are in knots. Come over here.'' He led her to the couch, and once she was comfortable, he knelt behind her and resumed the massage.

Jessica sighed as he rhythmically worked her shoulders and stroked her neck. The tension, as if absorbed through his fingertips, slipped away. With a murmured sound of pleasure, she let her head loll forward.

Clay pulled the pins from her hair and it tumbled to her shoulders, a curtain of sunshine-colored silk. The strands slipped over his fingers as he caressed and kneaded her scalp. Her scent was totally female, drawing him in with its subtlety, enveloping him with its power. He didn't shy away, but instead breathed deeply and let himself be surrounded.

He moved his hands down her back, along her spine. She moaned in response. The throaty sound was an instinctive invitation, and Clay's body tightened in response. Closing his eyes, he willed himself to relax.

"Tell me about your day," he murmured when he knew his voice wouldn't betray his need.

"Bill and I had another—" her lids fluttered up at the memory "—fight."

Her muscles tensed but he continued to work at them. "No, Jessica, don't tighten up. That's it, stay relaxed. Now tell me all about it."

Jessica concentrated on his hands as she spoke. "He's pressuring me about the cookie account. He wants to know what's holding us up."

"What did you tell him?"

"A partial truth." Jessica sighed with pleasure. Clay's touch, alternately forceful and playful, mesmerized her. "I told him the clients were disagreeing with one another, and that in all probability we'd have to do another presentation." Tension rippled through her. "He wasn't pleased."

"The massage won't do you any good if you tie yourself into knots again. We'll work this out."

"That's easy for you to say. You're not the one who was called incompetent." Hurt trembled in her voice, and she swore and swung around to face him. "No, you're still the golden boy of advertising; the screwup is entirely my fault."

Clay lifted his eyebrows. "Golden boy? Please, Jessica."

She slipped away from his hands and stood, her back to him. "Didn't you know? According to Bill Mann you can do no wrong." Her voice was brittle. "Father said he was considering taking me off the account. He doesn't think I'm ready for that much responsibility."

"Bastard," Clay muttered.

"If Monday morning's creative meeting doesn't go well, I'm off the account. I should have just gone along with your direction from the beginning and everything would have been fine." She pushed the hair out of her eyes. "It's too late now."

"No." Clay couldn't stand the defeat in her voice and turned her toward him. His gaze met and held hers. "Don't you see? It wouldn't have mattered if either of us had gone along with the other. If we'd presented only mine, Sandra would have objected; if we'd presented yours, Ty would have said 'No way.' In my opinion, we saved time by presenting two losers at once."

"You're right," she whispered. The truth of Clay's statement spilled over her like sunshine. The fact that neither direction would have been acceptable to both brother and sister hadn't crossed her mind before. She smiled. Her father was wrong. She hadn't acted unprofessionally. She was doing a good job.

Clay caught his breath. She was so lovely with her flushed cheeks and warm eyes. Her hair was wild from his fingers, her skirt rumpled, her blouse partially untucked. The ice princess was gone. This was the way he'd wanted to see her from that very first time when he'd seen her standing in the sun, an ice maiden impervious to heat. He'd wanted to see her warm, rumpled and touchable. He still wanted to see her the same way in his bed, welcoming him not just into her body, but into her heart.

His breath was trapped in his chest and he quickly, lightly, cupped her cheek. "I've got to go."

She took his hand with gentle fingers and cradled her face in his caress. Her eyes searched his, wondering at the sadness that lingered there. "Why?"

Clay slipped his hand from hers. "Because I need something you're not ready to give me. Good night, Jessica."

Six

Clay, wait!'' There was an edge of desperation in her voice. Jessica took a lurching step, then stopped and lowered her eyes. ''Tell me.'' She raised her eyes and drew a deep breath. ''Tell me . . . what you need.''

''I already did.''

''Yes.'' Jessica curled her stockinged toes into the carpeting. The fear was back. Her heart beat furiously against her chest, her breathing was shallow and painful. But there was something stronger than fear inside her. It pushed against her walls, it strained to be free. And as it did her heartbeat slowed and her breathing grew easy.

''I want you, Clay.'' She uncurled her toes as the words rushed past her lips. ''I want you to stay. I need to be with you.''

Arousal was immediate, overpowering. But he had to be sure. ''Are you being practical, Jessica?''

She took a step toward him. Freedom bubbled inside her; her laugh was husky and delighted. ''No.''

"This isn't a logical decision," he said softly, holding himself back when all he wanted to do was touch her.

She took another step and her body brushed against his. "No. This is most impractical. This borders on the irrational." She ran her hands up his chest until they rested on his shoulders. "But I don't care. I want you."

"You're sure?" He nipped at her upper lip; his tongue darted in to caress hers. "No regrets?" He pressed his lips to the pulse that was throbbing at the base of her throat. "No recriminations?"

Jessica plunged her fingers into his honey-colored hair and arched against him. "No, none," she murmured, her voice a throaty purr. "Clay...turn me to fire."

He laughed against her lips a moment before he captured them. Their tongues twined, tasted, urged. Clay suddenly felt like the barbarian she'd called him. He was wild for her. His need knew no civility, acknowledged no rules. He slipped his hands down and cupped her derriere, lifted her off the ground and rubbed her against him. When Jessica wrapped her legs around his middle, he groaned, diving his tongue deeper into her mouth, demanding everything she had, giving her everything in return.

Jessica shuddered as he moved her against himself and she felt the force of his arousal. How could she ever have thought Clay the wrong man for her? Could the wrong man make her feel as if she were flying without ever leaving the ground? Could he make her feel so totally female...so complete, if he wasn't right for her? She clung to him as he carried her to the bedroom.

Clay lowered her slowly to her feet. Her bedroom was cool, elegant and efficient. There was no hint here of the Jessica he now held in his arms, the Jessica who was unrestrained and ardent, the Jessica who was demanding things a cool woman never would.

He pushed the linen jacket from her shoulders. It caught on her watch and she helped him remove it. With a quick laugh she tossed the jacket across the room. When he fumbled with the tiny mother-of-pearl buttons on her blouse, she was the one who tugged.

Jessica felt the fabric give, heard it rend under her eager fingers, but didn't care. All she cared about was Clay—his touch, his heat, his freedom. There were no troublesome buttons on Clay's cotton pullover, and she yanked it over his head. She pulled on her skirt's zipper; the garment slipped off her hips and she kicked it out of the way.

She dropped her hands to the waistband of her slip and hose but found Clay already there, working at the clinging bits of silk and nylon. Both garments ended up as a delicate cushion under her feet.

Jessica arched her neck as he plundered the sensitive skin along the column of her throat, as he buried his head between her naked breasts. He whispered soft, hot words over her fevered skin. The sensation was incredible, and she moaned with pleasure.

Clay caught her moan against his lips, tasted its sweetness and dived deeper. Layer by layer her veneer had disappeared, revealing the woman he'd known would be there—a woman who was open and passionate and giving. He lowered her to the mattress.

Jessica accepted his weight with a sound of pleasure. His worn cords were fuzzy against her thighs and his belt buckle pressed into her abdomen. She breathed deeply, growing intoxicated on the scent of passion, its headiness numbing her. She ran her palms over his chest, marveling in the heat radiating from his skin, wondering if hers was the same, wanting the fire to take her.

It seemed an eternity before there was only his muscled flesh melding to her smooth, soft swells, before their mingled sighs at the contact.

Greedy for sensation, Clay touched, molded, explored. He found the curve of her breast enticing, the hard point exciting. Greedier still, he tasted, teased, urged. He wrote warm, wet messages on her abdomen, across her breasts, on the inside of her thigh. And he took pleasure in what had before been ordinary, the crook of an arm, the back of a knee, the arch of an eyebrow.

Jessica was just as impatient, just as ravenous. She discovered a warm, secret spot behind his ear that throbbed as she stroked it. She trailed her tongue along his shoulder, across his abdomen; salt clung to his skin and she delighted in its tingle. She asked, she urged and finally she opened herself to him. No walls, no reservations.

Their lips met, their fingers laced. For the second time that night, Jessica wrapped her legs around him. She clung until she had no more strength, until Clay's lips muffled her cries, until the black of the night was exchanged for the violet of dreams.

Sunlight streamed through the tilted slats of the blinds, creating long, narrow patches of light on the bed. Jessica's lids fluttered at the sting of light, awareness at first only tinting the fuzzy edges of consciousness, then seeping into and finally overtaking sleep. She gave it up reluctantly, lingering over her first sensations as she would linger later over her first cup of coffee.

Sitting up, Jessica pushed the tangle of hair out of her eyes and glanced at Clay. Still asleep, he lay on his stomach, one arm dangling off the side of the bed, his breathing deep and even. The sheet was caught at his waist and his body looked strong and bronzed against the delicate percale. She reached out to smooth his tousled hair, then drew back her hand, uncertain of herself and her own reactions.

Not wanting to wake him, she slipped cautiously out of bed and into her robe. She shoved her hands into its deep pockets and surveyed the disaster. Clothes were strewn crazily over the bedroom. A blush crept into her cheeks as she remembered the way she'd ripped hers from her body, then impatiently kicked them aside.

Her bra was at her feet and she stooped to pick it up. Jessica trailed a finger over the fabric, frowning as she did so. It was smooth, white and unadorned. Not an ugly brassiere, but not pretty either. Serviceable—she didn't like the word and pushed it away. Her frown deepened and her gaze drifted over the room in search of her panties. They were under the vanity and she knelt to retrieve them. They were the same as the bra—serviceable. This time she couldn't push the word away and she curled her fingers around the fabric as she stared at them.

Clay's eyes opened slowly. She was standing in a patch of sunlight. The brilliant light, the oversize robe, the wistfulness of her expression made her appear delicate, even ethereal. Her winter-white velour robe with its bell sleeves and gold stitching looked like a medieval ermine vestment... and she looked like royalty. Clay's lips twitched. He'd thought her a princess the first time he saw her, and he thought so still.

But the frown bothered him. "What's wrong, Jessica?" he asked, his voice husky with sleep.

Jessica whirled around, still clutching the bits of fabric. Clay was sitting up in bed, watching her. His question had violated the stillness as a pebble disturbs a glassy pond, rippling over her in ever widening, disturbing circles. "You awaken quietly," she murmured.

"Yes." He lowered his eyes to her hands, then returned them to her face. "Jessica?"

She made a small, nervous sound. "Nothing...it's silly, I..." Her teeth caught her bottom lip and she looked away. After a moment she spoke, her words a fierce whisper. "Never again, Clay. Serviceable isn't good enough."

He stiffened at her words, unsure of her meaning. "What are you saying?"

Her eyes met his and she dropped the undergarments onto the bed in front of him. "They're so plain. That isn't the way I feel...it isn't the way I want you to see me."

Clay pushed away the sheet and got out of bed. He stepped nearer, but didn't touch her. "Oh, Jess—"

"There must have been lots of women." Her chin wavered ever so slightly and she cleared her throat. "Women who wore red, and lace, and totally sheer. Women who—" His kiss captured her words, stole her breath. Her head fell back, and she held his arms for support. When he pulled away, her lids fluttered up.

There was surprise in her eyes, and passion, and vulnerability. It was the last that touched him most. "You're so beautiful, Jess. You don't need any trappings."

"No?" Jessica whispered, her voice breathy and feminine. It was amazing to her the way he could soothe, could reassure with just a few words. And the little girl in her wanted—needed—reassurance.

"No." His eyes roamed over her. "Don't you know that I'd rather feast my eyes on one of your smiles than a thousand perfect sunsets? That I'd rather drink of your lips than of the finest champagne, would rather hold you in my arms for one moment than a thousand women wearing red lace forever?"

Her pulse fluttered both at his words and at the way his eyes glowed as he looked at her. She suddenly felt beautiful—beautiful and exotic.

"I wouldn't change anything about you," he murmured, untying her robe and pushing it slowly off her shoulders.

She let it fall, finding the way it whispered down her body erotic. She felt like a goddess, a siren, a totally sexual being. As the garment pooled at her feet, she sighed in anticipation of her flesh melding to his.

"Ah, Jess..." He trailed his fingers over her collarbone, shoulders, breasts; following with his tongue—and creating warm, wet paths on her skin. "You taste like cream, and I'd choose cream over confection every time."

A moan caught in her throat as he took the tip of one breast into his mouth, then the other. Her fingers curled into his hair as he dipped his tongue into her navel, as he alternated tiny kisses and teasing nips along her abdomen, hips, thighs. Pleasure quivered through her as he parted the soft, blond curls and tasted all of her.

A sound of passion shuddered past her lips. Jessica's knees buckled and they both sank to the floor.

Clay made love to her slowly, thoughtfully. Gone was the frenzy of the night before. Now he touched places he'd missed in the rush, told her things he'd only hinted at, took time to arouse where there'd been no time before.

An hour ago Jessica had thought the stroking of the crisp sheets against her nudity a pleasure to linger over—now that sensation was negligible compared to Clay's stroking inside her. She'd thought the morning sun blinding, but it paled before the way she felt at this moment.

She tightened her arms around him and called his name. Clay answered her. Her name sounded unbelievably sweet upon his lips. She soared, reaching for the heavens and beyond, Clay by her side. And as she touched a place that was warm and brilliant and shattering, she heard Clay's release.

The trip back was slow and easy. Her breathing evened, her heart steadied, her flesh cooled. Jessica smiled languidly up at him.

Clay propped himself on one elbow and watched her yawn and stretch. Her eyes were sleepy from loving, her hair was a tangle of blond silk. He caught several of the shining strands and rubbed them between his fingers. She was so beautiful...so special. She called to him in ways no woman ever had, touched him in places he hadn't even known existed. He wanted her now; he wanted her tomorrow.

But what of the day after that? She was the wrong woman for him. Their goals were as different as spring and winter. He wanted the freedom to travel, to experience other places, other ways of life. And she wanted a career, with all the chains that definition imposed. He'd tried it her way before—it'd almost killed him. And she wouldn't change.

Jessica frowned as she felt the intensity of his gaze. His eyes were sad and she was suddenly afraid. "What are you thinking?"

That I'll miss you, he thought, tenderly brushing the wisps of hair away from her face. Instead, he said, "I was thinking how beautiful you are."

Her eyes searched his, wanting to believe him but not quite being able to. Willing away her unease, she smiled and walked her fingers slowly up his chest. "Is that all? I like compliments."

Her coquetry was unexpected and charming. "I'm sure you do." He pulled her on top of him, sliding his hands down the gentle arch of her back to cup her bottom. "But you'll have to do without."

Jessica lifted an eyebrow. "You sleep with a guy once—"

"Twice." He nuzzled her lips.

"And they treat you like old loafers."

"Loafers?"

"Mmm..." She nipped his neck. "Old loafers with holes in the soles. No flowers, no candy, no romance. Disgusting, Clay." She wriggled against him. "Really disgusting."

Arousal was instantaneous and Clay groaned. What was disgusting was that he wanted her again. He was crazy for her. How could he think of leaving when he couldn't do without her for an hour? Giving in to his need, he caught her lips. It was a long, slow, thorough meeting. When he pulled away, she was breathless.

"Come to the beach house with me," Clay whispered. "Tonight I want to make love to you under the stars, with the sound of the ocean in my ears, the warm wind against my back." He caught her lips again, teased her tongue with the tip of his. "And tomorrow I want to stay in bed. I want to watch old Cary Grant movies, eat popcorn and drink champagne . . . make love. I want to fall asleep with you in my arms. Spend the weekend with me, Jess.''

There was a strange fluttering in her chest. It made her warm, slightly dizzy. "I'd like that," she murmured, tangling her fingers in his hair. "But first I'd like this." She caught his mouth in a searing kiss.

Hours later, Jessica thumbed through the copy she was proofing in disgust. Clay had gone to buy groceries alone so she could get her work out of the way. She hadn't gotten much done, unless she considered staring into space and daydreaming about Clay getting work done. She lowered her gaze determinedly to the papers in front of her. They blurred before her eyes, being replaced by a picture of herself and Clay making love. A soft smile touched her lips. He was wonderful, made her feel wonderful.

She couldn't believe what a fool she'd been, fighting having an affair with him. She slipped off her glasses and thoughtfully tapped them on the stack of papers. Maybe they were even having a relationship. Sure. After all, it wasn't purely sexual—they were colleagues and friends. This relationship made a lot of sense; in fact, it fitted very well into her life. They went to the same office every morning, they could work on the cookie account at home at night, but—she wrinkled her nose—maybe she was jumping the gun here. He'd asked her to spend this weekend with him, not the next six. It wouldn't do to take things for granted or to act as though she wanted this to be a permanent arrangement. Because she didn't; the last thing she wanted was commitment. She would handle this affair—relationship—like a mature, worldly woman. No problem.

Hearing a car door slam, she jumped up and raced to the window. It was Clay, juggling three bags of groceries. A brilliant smile lit her face as she threw open the door and ran outside to help him. "Hi." She took a bag from his hands, then peeked over the top. "Any good stuff?"

"Lots." He leaned over to give her a quick kiss, catching the edge of her smile. "Did you get much work done?"

Jessica hedged, not wanting him to know she'd been mooning over him. "Mmm...sure, of course."

"Great." Clay shifted the weight of the bags as he carried them inside. "Now we can go out and play."

"Mmm." Jessica's eyes slid guiltily to the waiting stack of papers. She really did need to sort through that mess before Monday, but she could work later this afternoon, or all day tomorrow. She had plenty of time.

"What did you have in mind?" Jessica asked, depositing the bag on the kitchen counter.

"Something crazy, something borderline illegal, definitely immoral."

Jessica laughed and shook her head. "Sounds interesting."

"What's interesting," Clay murmured, catching her hands, "is that outfit." His eyes skimmed over her, taking in the straight leg jeans, the oversize cotton pullover that fell off one shoulder, her bare feet. Her face was free of cosmetics, her hair, still damp from a shower, hung loose.

A little embarrassed by his inspection, she shifted her weight.

Clay drew her closer. "You look great. I especially like this neckline," he murmured, placing a string of loving nibbles along her shoulder.

"Oh..." Jessica tipped her head to one side, exposing more of her neck and shoulder. "Ali picked it out. She insisted and..." Her words trailed off as she gave herself up to his touch.

"I'll have to thank her next time I see her," Clay said, slipping his hands under the pullover to caress her bare flesh. He cupped her breasts and groaned as the nipples pressed into his palms. "Ah, Jess..." He gave her one final nuzzle before he set her away. "The Eskimo pies are melting."

Jessica laughed. "You're crazy."

"Yeah, but it's your fault." He stuck the ice-cream pies in the freezer.

"Mine?" Her eyebrows shot up innocently.

"Mmm-hmm. I was a perfectly normal advertising executive until you started driving me crazy." Clay ignored her choking sound and shook his head sadly. "You're worse than a four-martini lunch, Jess."

"Insanity's a sad thing," she murmured, her lips twitching. "Such a hard body, such a soft brain."

"Come over here and I'll show you a hard body."

When he crooked his finger and wiggled his eyebrows, Jessica laughed and started unpacking a bag loaded with junk food. "Don't you eat anything nutritious?" Her voice was incredulous as she pulled out the third kind of chip snack.

"That's what weekends are for, Jess, eating stuff that's bad for you, not getting enough sleep, being a lazy, unproductive member of society." He half folded, half crumpled the brown paper bags and shoved them under the counter, then laughed at her exasperated expression. "I left something in the car. Wait here."

Jessica took out the bags again and began refolding them. She shook her head and sighed. She was just as productive on the weekends as during the week, maybe more so. And she made sure she ate well, got plenty of sleep and exercise to make up for what she might have missed during the week. Bending over, she stacked the neatly creased, flattened bags next to the cleaning solutions. He really was crazy, she decided with another small shake of her head.

The front door slammed. A moment later Clay walked into the kitchen carrying a large, flat package. Jessica eyed the brown-paper-wrapped parcel curiously. "What's this?"

"It's for you." He propped it against the counter.

"For me?" she repeated, surprised. "What is it?"

"Why don't you open it and find out?"

"Well...okay."

Clay found her obvious fluster charming. Shoving his hands into the back pockets of his jeans, he rocked on his heels, watching her expectantly. She knelt and began loosening the taped edges. Clay grinned; she approached unwrapping a package the way she approached everything else, carefully and methodically.

Jessica's fingers trembled as she released the last piece of tape. With an uncharacteristic burst of impatience, she ripped aside the paper and her breath came out as a surprised squeak. Color and energy and life poured from the revealed canvas, and Jessica's widened eyes met Clay's.

She was surprised. Clay smiled, liking having caught her off guard. "I wanted you to have it," he said simply.

Her pulse raced. She remained where she was, kneeling in front of the painting, staring up at Clay. After a moment she said, "I don't know what to say."

His dimples appeared. "How about thank you?"

"Oh, yes...of course." Her eyes returned to the painting. She trailed a finger reverently along the frame. The painting was so alive, so powerful. How had Clay known she'd been unable to forget it? How had he known that every time she looked at the peaceful little landscape she'd purchased instead, she'd thought of this one?

She cleared her throat, suddenly tight with tears. "Thank you," she murmured, standing. She wrapped her arms around his middle and pressed her cheek to his chest. "I love it."

"I'm glad." He ran his fingers through her silky hair. "Where are you going to hang it?"

She tipped back her head and laughed up at him. It was a husky, sensual sound. "Can't you guess, Clay? I'm going to hang it above the bed."

"You're a vixen, Ms. Mann."

"Mmm-hmm." She slipped her hands under his UCLA sweatshirt and stroked his back. "Plan to do anything about it?" Clay's answer was shockingly intimate and Jessica gasped and sagged against him.

Seven

"Go away," Jessica mumbled, turning from the annoying voice. She curled into a sleepy ball, crushing the pillow into her face.

"Come on, sleepyhead, wake up." Clay climbed noisily onto the bed and straddled her. "I have coffee," he coaxed. "And breakfast."

Jessica rolled onto her back and looked up at him through squinting eyes. "Why are you doing this to me? What have I done to deserve this cruel treatment?"

Clay planted a kiss on her nose. "It's time to get up, grouchy one. The day's getting away from us."

"Right now, I'd like to get away from you." Her scowl deepened. "Why are you so cheerful? How can you be so awake?" She pulled the pillow back over her face. "It's barely dawn."

"It's barely noon." Clay pulled away the pillow, grinning as she groaned and blinked. "Capable and efficient

Jessica, I've never seen you so sluggish. This is really blow-
ing my image of you.''

Jessica rubbed her eyes and pulled herself into a sitting
position. ''What was that drink called, and how many did I
have?''

''A boilermaker.'' Clay's lips twitched at her horrified
expression. ''I didn't count. You couldn't have had too
many or you wouldn't have been able to stay on the mechanical bull as long as you did.''

''Mechanical bull?'' she repeated in a squeaky voice. The
whole, wild evening was coming back to her. No wonder
she'd wanted to stay in bed—she'd had too little sleep, too
much to drink and was mortified at her own behavior.

''Uh-huh.'' His tone was conciliatory. ''Too bad they
kicked us out before you got your prize.''

''No more, Clay.'' Jessica covered her ears. ''I lived it, I
don't want to hear about it.''

Clay's grin widened. ''I still can't believe you picked a
fight with a two-hundred-and-fifty-pound cowboy. Tossed
your drink right in his face. But I think you were completely justified. After all, he did try to grab your—''

''Stop!'' She sagged against the pillows. ''Coffee, Clay. I
need coffee now.''

Clay laughed and poured her a cup. ''It wasn't as bad as
all that, Jess.''

''No, it was worse. I feel as if I'm going to die.'' She shot
him an accusing glance. ''And it's all your fault.''

''Yeah.'' He briefly caught her lips, then grinned against
them. ''But I brought you coffee...and breakfast.''

Jessica returned his smile, nipping at his lower lip before
he could pull away. ''I'm suddenly starving.'' She shifted on
the bed, making room for a tray. ''What did you make?''

His eyes crinkled at the corners and he touched a finger
to her lips. ''Don't move.'' He hurried across the room, returning with a tray, complete with linen napkins, a bud vase

and the Sunday paper. He placed it in front of her. "Ta-da!"

Jessica stared at the tray in disbelief. "Cookies?" she murmured, lifting her eyes to his. "You brought me cookies? For breakfast?"

"Not just any cookies. Cookies from Heaven."

A fluttering laugh escaped her. "Clay, that's really—"

"Trashy?" Clay supplied. "Decadent?"

"Mmm-hmm." Jessica rubbed her hands together. "But so yummy."

Clay pinched her. "Don't get greedy, princess. Scoot over and give me a chance."

She lifted her chin and grinned wickedly. "Like you need..." The words died on her lips; her expression grew blank. "Oh, my God!"

Clay stiffened. "Jess, what's wrong? Are you—?"

"That's it, Clay!" Jessica tossed aside the covers, jumped out of bed and faced him. "I know it'll work!" She pushed the tangle of hair out of her eyes. "Don't you see, that's it!"

Clay leaned back against the pillows and grinned. "I see plenty, Jess...." His eyes skimmed over her body, nude and still flushed with sleep. "But I suspect you're referring to something else."

His comment nonplussed her—but for only a moment. She flew across the room and into her robe, all the while continuing her dialogue. "Why didn't we see it? It's perfect!"

Clay laughed. "Clue me in, Jess. I'm not following you."

"The campaign, the cookies." She began to pace. "Think of our playful bantering of a moment ago. Think of our conversation on the beach the first time we ate Cookies from Heaven."

Clay's smile was slow and delighted. "I'm getting it. Go on."

"Picture this..." She paused, dragging her hands through her hair as she thought. "Sunday morning, a young couple having breakfast in bed. They're attractive, obviously living the good life, in love. The tone's light and teasing, the repartee is witty.''

Clay stood, poured himself a cup of coffee and began munching on a cookie. ''Light is spilling through the windows, there's a gentle breeze stirring the curtains. Okay, we've got the mood. What are the lines?''

Jessica drew her eyebrows together. ''How about this? 'Good morning, darling. I brought you breakfast.' The man whisks away a linen napkin with a flourish. 'Ta-da!'''

''The woman,'' Clay chimed in, ''looks at her lover disapprovingly. 'Cookies for breakfast? Really, Steven.'''

'''Not any cookies,' he says. 'Cookies from Heaven.'''

Clay's eyes met Jessica's. Hers were dancing with the excitement he felt. ''They say the same thing we just did, because it's natural. It *is* decadent to eat cookies for breakfast—there's no nutrition, it's total junk food—''

''Parents would die before they'd let their children eat cookies for breakfast, but adults love being bad—splurging, indulging themselves.'' Jessica laughed out loud. ''Look at the way we behaved last night.... Look at what you brought me for breakfast. We can sell that, Clay. We can sell the sensation of being slightly naughty, a little irresponsible, a tad decadent.''

''I like it.'' Clay passed her a cup of coffee and the plate of cookies, snitching the biggest as he did so. ''The couple playfully fight over a cookie, say a peanut butter and chocolate chip, they laugh in unison and decide to share.''

''See what I mean?'' Jessica clapped her hands together. ''It's perfect. There can be a tag line like: 'It's always the right time for Cookies from Heaven.'''

''How about this?'' Clay interjected. '''Go ahead, splurge. Cookies from Heaven.' No wait—'' Clay stopped pacing and stared for a moment at the ceiling. He lowered his eyes to hers and his delivery was dramatic. ''You love being decadent—indulge yourself. Cookies from Heaven.''

"I love it! This is good stuff, Clay. Really good." Jessica couldn't contain the elation in her voice. She crossed to the window, stared out at the beach, then swung back toward Clay. "We can do a series of television spots, all with the same mood. In one, the couple can be on the beach, laughing and teasing like they do in the Sunday morning spot. Another could take place over an intimate candlelight dinner, maybe another at the airport."

"We could make a play for the teenage market. The mood could be similar but upbeat. Listen to this—a teenage boy buys his girlfriend Cookies from Heaven instead of flowers or candy. Tag line: 'Indulge her—Cookies from Heaven.'"

Jessica held out her hands to stop him, practically dancing with enthusiasm. "No, even better, a teenage girl buys the boy she's trying to win Cookies from Heaven—"

"A play on 'The way to a man's heart is through his stomach.'"

"Right. Oh, Clay..." Jessica ran across the room and threw her arms around his neck. "We've done it! I know both clients will love it! I know it! Say you think so too." She pinched him playfully. "Say it—"

"Yes, the clients will love it." Laughing, Clay lifted her high in the air and swung her around. "I think it's wonderful, fabulous."

She joined in his laughter until she was giddy with it. "Stop, Clay, I can't breathe." When he lowered her, she rested her forehead against his chest and breathed deeply. He'd already showered, and smelled like the spicy soap he favored. Jessica pressed closer, finding herself aroused by the familiar scent. She moved her hands from his shoulders until she could feel his steady heartbeat under her palm and all she could think about was ripping the covering of his shirt away.

Jessica looked up at him seductively. "Clay..." She moistened her lips, her voice deepened. "I think we should celebrate."

"Oh?"

"We deserve it," she murmured, smiling to herself at his increased heartbeat under her palm, at the darkening of his eyes. Standing on tiptoe, she tasted his neck with the tip of her tongue. "In fact, since you brought the cookies, I think I should supply the party."

"You think so, do you?" Clay slipped his hands under the closing of her robe to cup her breasts. He groaned as she teasingly stepped away from his hands.

"Oh yes, fair's fair, you know." Her smile was wicked as she unbelted the robe and tossed it aside. "I didn't have time to send out an invitation; I hope you don't have a previous engagement." As she spoke she sauntered toward the bed.

Clay jerked his shirt over his head and kicked off his shoes. "Sorry, I have back-to-back appointments all day."

Jessica curled into a provocative position on the bed. "Break them."

The mattress sagged under Clay's weight. Their eyes met.

"You got it," Clay whispered, then took her mouth in an enveloping kiss.

Monday morning found Jessica panicky. If her father didn't like their proposal, she would be off the account and everything she'd worked for would be lost. She tugged at the sleeve of her jacket, smoothed her skirt, then scowled at her reflection. "I wish I'd brought something more business-like to wear."

Clay eyed her two-piece suit with amusement. It was tailored and conservative. "What's wrong with what you have on?" he asked, knotting his fire engine-red tie.

She expelled a breath loudly and threw her hands up. "It's pink, for God's sake! I never wear a pastel to a formal meeting—it's too feminine. And the last thing I want to do is remind Father that I'm a woman." She glanced back at the mirror. "Damn."

"It's not pink, it's mauve," Clay murmured, coming up behind her and gently massaging her shoulders. "And you're nervous."

Jessica shut her eyes and leaned against him. "Yes."

"We both know our ideas are perfect for this account. We also know the clients are going to love them." He touched his lips to her hair. "There's nothing to be nervous about."

"For you." Jessica twisted to look up at him. "Father was serious when he said he'd take the account away from me if this meeting didn't go well. I have this feeling he just wants me off the account and will do anything to see that happens. I don't know why, or how he'll do it—"

"Why would Bill have hired you away from Ad House if he didn't trust your ability? Above all, your father's a businessman. Trust me, he won't rock the boat."

Jessica frowned. "Everything you just said makes sense, but I have this feeling—"

"I have a feeling too, Jess." He pulled her against him, his laughter stirred her hair. "And I warn you—" he nipped her earlobe "—it makes me crazy."

Jessica smiled up at him. "If you're trying to distract me, it's working."

"I'd like to totally distract you, but I'm afraid we haven't time." He kissed the tip of her nose before stepping away.

"No, we don't." Her tone was laced with regret.

"Shall we?"

With one last longing glance at the bed, she straightened her shoulders. "Yes." Jessica picked up her briefcase, sighing as she thought of the stack of still-untouched papers inside and of the hours it would take her to go through them. With a wan smile at Clay, she headed down the stairs.

The Mann Agency's conference table was littered with Styrofoam cups, fast food wrappers and overflowing ashtrays; a haze from too many smokers cooped up in one room hung in the air. Jessica's smile was easy and her eyes circled the table as she spoke. Her hands were casually shoved into her oversize jacket pockets, and she was grateful for the way they concealed her white knuckles. As if sensing her tension, Clay briefly, but reassuringly touched her shoulder. His touch was magic—her fingers unclenched, the knot in her chest eased.

"Clay and I would like everyone's gut reaction to the creative direction I've just outlined. Consider this a rush job. We need everyone's input and everyone's time." Her eyes lighted on her father; his expression was unreadable. She took a deep breath and continued. "It'll be a long forty-eight hours, but I'd like to present a total package to the clients Wednesday morning. Are there any questions?"

There was a moment of nerve-racking silence before a flutter of applause went around the table. Jessica released her pent-up breath at the same moment everyone stood and began talking. Within moments she and Clay were surrounded, their backs were being slapped, their hands clasped and shook.

"Jess, Clay, a stroke of genius. You've got my total support."

"Wonderful! We'll win a Clio with this one. Good going, guys."

"Jessica," Liz, the copywriter, whispered as she nudged her, "I'm itching to get going on this, if there's nothing else—"

Before Jessica could answer, Clay pulled her into his arms and caught her lips in a quick, hard kiss. Her eyes widened in surprise, her hands flattened against his chest. "What are you doing?" she hissed.

"What do you think?" he asked, amused.

Behind her Liz giggled and Jessica stiffened in Clay's arms. "Let me go. Now." As she pushed against his chest, the muscles under her palms bunched. Their eyes tangled. His were filled with challenge, and a prickling sensation raced up her spine. "Damn it, Clay," she muttered, realizing he meant to kiss her again. "Let me—" His lips swallowed her words.

A moment later she was free. Reining in her anger, she straightened her jacket and stepped coolly aside. "Go ahead, Liz, get started. Plan on conferring later this afternoon." When Liz scurried away, she turned back to Clay. She worked to maintain a crisp, businesslike tone, but knew her eyes smoldered with fury. "We need to start lining up talent for the television spots. You know what we're looking for. Pull out all the head sheets and narrow it down to twenty or twenty-five men and women. Contact them and we'll make appointments for a cattle call. Now, excuse me." She turned to leave.

Before she could do so, Clay grabbed her elbow and swung her back around. She lowered her eyes to the place where his fingers bit into her flesh, then raised them to his face. A muscle twitched in his jaw and he looked as if he could happily strangle her.

"What's the matter, Jess? Afraid Daddy will know you're human?"

The need to hit him came upon her so suddenly that it took her breath away. "Don't start this. Not now, not here."

"Then when, Jessica?" His eyes pinned hers. "Should I call Barbara and make an appointment? Maybe I can touch you at eight o'clock Thursday evening. Perhaps you'd even have time for—"

Dear God, Jessica thought, her gaze flying to her father's formidable expression, *here he comes.* "Stop it, Clay," she pleaded. "Please stop."

Clay bit back his words and released her arm. "We'll talk later," he murmured, then nodding at Bill Mann, turned and walked away.

Jessica watched him for a moment, then faced her father. Desperately holding on to her composure, she forced calm into her voice. "So, Bill, do you have anything to add to our proposal?"

Bill's eyes bored into hers. "What was that all about?"

"What? Oh, Clay." She shrugged. "Nothing at all."

"He kissed you."

"Yes." Annoyance rippled through her. She checked her watch. "I have a lot going on today, so if there's nothing else—"

He caught her arm. "Don't get involved with him, Jessica. It wouldn't be professional."

She was suddenly more than annoyed. "My professionalism isn't in question here. I've never conducted myself any way but professionally, and I resent the implication."

"Jessica, you know how these creative types are. They're not for us."

His tone was subtly condescending and only the breathlessness of fury kept her silent. Just for a moment. Using her most incisive tone and iciest stare, she said, "I'm sure I don't know what you mean, Father. Now, I really have to get to work. Excuse me."

Jessica strode from the conference room, so furious she was certain smoke was curling from her ears. If not there, surely from the words she muttered under her breath. She stalked into her office, slamming the door behind her.

Moments later she was flipping sightlessly through the stack of papers on her desk, still cursing under her breath. Men! She didn't know which was worse, Clay's flamboyant public show of affection or her father's nosy, narrow-minded concern. Why couldn't they both just leave her alone and let her do her job?

"Jess—er, Jessica, I hate to disturb you...." Barbara's voice trailed off.

"But you will, anyway," Jessica said wearily. "Come in, Barbara, I won't bite."

The receptionist didn't look convinced. "It's just that... you looked so busy."

A grin touched the corners of Jessica's mouth. "Looked so angry, you mean." Laughter sparkled in Barbara's eyes, and the grin widened. "What's that?" she asked, eyeing the brightly wrapped box in Barbara's hands.

"It came for you." Cautiously she set it on the desk.

Jessica looked at it, then lifted concerned eyes to Barbara's. "There are holes punched in the top."

"I know." Amusement lurked in the receptionist's voice. "That's why I brought it right in."

It was from Clay, of course. Jessica tentatively pulled it toward her. In light of their last conversation and considering Clay's wacky sense of humor, she was unsure whether she wanted to open it. "Holes in the box," she repeated. "I don't think that's a good sign. Do you?"

"Not really." Barbara perched on the edge of the desk, obviously unwilling to leave until the contents of the package were revealed. "Maybe you'd better open the card first."

"Good idea." Jessica slit open the envelope, pulled out the card, then read it aloud. "This is Fred. He reminded me of you." She reminded Clay of someone—named Fred?

"You might as well open it. After all, Fred's waiting."

"I guess so." Jessica took a deep breath, tore away the wrapping and lifted the lid of the box.

It was a turtle. A small, green turtle in a glass bowl. It lumbered the way all turtles do, craning its neck as it moved across the gravel. Jessica's surprised eyes met Barbara's. "Do I look like a turtle to you?"

"No way, Jessica. A blond mink, maybe, but certainly not a turtle," Barbara laughed as she slid off the edge of the desk and headed toward the door. "I'd better get back to my post. Liz hates answering the phone."

"Thanks for bringing it." Jessica lowered her eyes to the glass bowl. She tilted her head, lightly touching Fred's shell with her index finger. He was cute. Clumsy and awkward, but endearing nevertheless.

Of course, she'd never likened herself to a turtle, nor could she fathom why Clay would, but she was touched. Silly man, he could think of the sweetest things to do.

Jessica moved the bowl aside and settled back into her chair. If only he wouldn't kiss her in conference rooms—a smile tugged at her mouth—at least when there were other people around. She shook her head. He really didn't play fair; staying irritated with him was an impossible feat. She glanced back at Fred, her expression soft and amused.

"My, my, don't you look like the cat who swallowed the canary." Ali swept into the office.

Jessica's head jerked up and she automatically straightened her shoulders. "Ali, what are you doing here?"

"Bugging Daddy." She laughed and flopped into the chair opposite Jessica.

Jessica's eyebrows rose. "Oh?"

"Mmm, I hit him for a loan. It gets his Type A personality all in a huff."

Jessica hid a grin as she rocked back in her chair. "Ali, if you needed money, you could have asked me."

"Yeah, I know." Her eyes settled curiously on the turtle. "Mom would have lent me some, too, but it drives Daddy so crazy...I couldn't resist."

This time Jessica wasn't as successful; a fluttering laugh escaped from behind her hand. She cleared her throat. "You're such a devil."

Ali's eyes brightened with interest. "That snicker was most un-Jessica-like. What's up?"

Jessica ignored the question. "You shouldn't be broke. Didn't you just finish a big job for the Elmwood Corporation?"

"They've been billed." She jerked her head toward the fishbowl. "What's that?"

Jessica couldn't resist the obvious. "It's a turtle. His name is Fred."

Ali peered into the bowl. "He's kinda cute."

"That depends on your frame of reference." Jessica's tone was dry. "You wouldn't want to date him, would you?"

"Mmm, I suppose not." Ali met her sister's eyes. "Although I'd always thought you'd enjoy having a pet, keeping a turtle in your office is also most un-Jessica-like. Care to tell me what's going on?"

Just as Jessica opened her mouth to assure her sister that nothing was going on, Clay strode into the room. She could tell he was still angry and silently groaned. She wasn't in the mood for a confrontation—especially in front of her sister.

"Ali," Clay said, nodding in her direction. "How was Vegas?"

"Profitable," Ali answered, lifting one perfect eyebrow. "And how was the soufflé?"

"Untouched."

Jessica stiffened. "Don't either of you have work to do?"

Clay set his jaw. "All the business I have right now is with you."

"Can't this wait?" Jessica moved her head slightly in her sister's direction.

"No. You and I are going to talk . . . now."

Ali's eyes flew from one to the other. A smile curved her lips and she stood. "Besides stopping by to ruin Daddy's day, I wanted to tell you I'll be out of town for a couple of months. I got a big commission in San Francisco. The Roosevelt Hotel."

"Oh, Ali, that's wonderful!" Jessica beamed at her sister.

"Congratulations." Clay tipped an imaginary hat.

"Thanks. I'm tickled, too; it's my biggest project yet. I also wanted to remind you that Mother's show at Gallery 3501 opens a week from Saturday." When Jessica opened her mouth to make an excuse, Ali added sternly, "You promised, Jessica. This is the most important night of her career. Don't ruin it for her."

Clay's eyes moved from one woman to the other. Ali's expression was determined; Jessica's was tight, her cheeks bright with color.

Silence stretched between the two. When Jessica spoke, her voice was low and sad. "A promise is a promise. I'll be there, Ali."

Relief washed over Ali's features. "Thanks, Sissy. It means a lot to her...and to me." A sudden grin lightened her tone. "See you both at the opening—I gotta go. Ciao."

They watched her leave, then turned to one another. Clay was the first to speak. "What was that all about?"

"Nothing." She gestured vaguely. "There's something else I want to talk to you about."

"You and Ali grew up with different parents, didn't you?"

Jessica made a sound of frustration. "Yes. Your behavior this morning—"

"Do you see your mother often?" Clay propped himself against the window casing and stared down at the street.

"No. Anyway, I'd like to clarify my position—"

"Why not?"

Jessica took a deep breath. "Why not what?"

"Why don't you see your mother?" He pushed away from the window and crossed to her. Their eyes met and held.

Her chin tilted. "I'm talking about your behavior this morning."

"And I'm talking about you."

"We either discuss this proclivity of yours for public affection, or we don't talk at all." Jessica folded her arms and waited.

Clay's eyes narrowed at the ultimatum. "What? You want me to promise not to kiss you in front of Daddy again?"

Her fingers clenched. "This isn't about my father."

"Oh? Maybe you'd better fill me in." He lowered his voice dangerously and took a step toward her. "What is this about?"

Her heart thundered in her chest, but her voice was crisp as she said, "It's necessary for me to separate my professional and private life. In my position I have to delegate responsibility; and I can't afford to have my authority questioned. I have to be taken seriously, Clay."

"Is that so? And where do I fit in, Jessica? Are we lovers... or are we nothing?"

Jessica's breath caught and she cleared her throat. "We... outside the office we're lovers. But when I'm working, I'm a vice-president." She moved to the window and stared out at the cloudless sky. "I don't want anyone to know about us... about our affair. No more gifts arriving at the office, no more embraces in front of the staff. I'm sure everyone's already speculating, but they're not certain. If they were, in one moment I'd go from vice-president to Clay's lover. I won't have that."

"Doesn't it matter what I want?" He was angry with her damned code of professionalism, with his own inability to sway her. "How far does this secrecy extend? You were uncomfortable in front of Ali. Your own sister! Am I only good in the dark, Jessica? Is that it?"

She spun around, eyes wide with shock. "You don't understand—"

"No, it's *you* who don't understand. I won't sneak around like what we're doing is sleazy."

"I'm sorry." She reached out a hand to touch him, then pulled it away. "I didn't mean you to feel that way. You knew who I was before we became involved."

"Yes, I knew." His voice deepened. "Do you know why Fred reminded me of you?"

"No."

Catching her chin with gentle fingers, he forced her gaze to his. "Because your center is as soft as his. And as vulnerable.'' When she opened her mouth to protest, he placed a finger against her lips. ''And, like Fred, you wear that damn piece of armor around you. It fools most . . . but not me.''

''Oh, Clay.'' Jessica took a deep breath; it seemed there wasn't enough oxygen in the room. She felt somehow different, as if she stood outside herself, looking at and listening to a stranger.

She was changing. Acknowledging that truth made her afraid, but she did so nevertheless. A month ago she would have vehemently denied being any of those things; she would have been irritated—even angry—with him for suggesting them. But today she was both touched and sad. When she spoke, her voice reflected her jumbled emotions. ''I can't say that I don't feel wonderful when you say things like that, nor can I deny that part of me wishes they were true. But I'm afraid you're seeing me the way you want me to be rather than as I really am. I'm steady and serious, a hard worker and a shrewd businesswoman. I lead a no-nonsense life filled with no-nonsense people.''

''You're the one who doesn't see reality, Jessica. For years you've tried so hard to be only one thing that that's all you think you are.''

''I don't have the time to argue with you. Nor do I have the energy to think up new ways of convincing you.'' She shook her head, looked away, then met his eyes once more. ''I need your promise that when we're at work we behave as colleagues, nothing more. Can you make me that promise, Clay?''

His eyes narrowed. It was his turn to deliver an ultimatum. ''On one condition.''

Jessica's eyebrows arched. ''And what would that be?''

''You tell me about your mother.''

''You never give up, do you?'' Jessica sighed and sank back into her chair. ''Oh, all right. But not now; we have too much going on. I'll tell you after the Cookies from Heaven presentation. Will that be satisfactory?"

Clay's eyes crinkled at the corners. That she was annoyed with him was evidenced by the crispness of her tone and the coolness of her eyes. "Okay, princess, it's a date." He paused at the door. "Cattle call is tomorrow morning at nine. Barbara's calling the talent. If you're curious, head sheets are on her desk."

Jessica watched him leave, then with a determined sigh, returned to her stack of papers.

The elevator was so crowded that she could feel the rumble of Clay's restrained laughter against her back. Jessica held her breath and fought back a smile of pure delight. Her palms were sweating, but only slightly, and she gripped the portfolio handles more tightly. The elevator doors slid open and Jessica and Clay stepped off, turning to watch as the doors closed. Their eyes met with a smile.

Jessica dropped her briefcase and portfolio, then threw her arms around Clay's neck. "They loved it! I knew they would, I knew it!"

Clay hugged her back, his laughter mingling with hers, the sound echoing in the deserted parking garage. "Yeah, and even better, they agreed with each other."

"Right. They both agreed we're brilliant."

"And we are." Clay collected her bags and handed them to her. His grin widened. "She only called him a Neanderthal once."

"Mmm-hmm, and he only called her a feminist fish-face twice." Jessica unlocked the passenger door, then tossed him the keys. "You drive. I'm too euphoric for the rules of the road."

Clay's eyes twinkled, but he didn't comment on her behavior. "Just as well. We have reservations at Gregory's."

"Reservations?" Jessica's brow wrinkled. "For what?"

Clay started the car. "For lunch, of course."

"But the service is so slow at Gregory's, it'll take all afternoon. I have work—"

"You've done nothing but work for forty-eight hours. We both deserve a treat. Besides, we should celebrate. We sold our idea, one idea, to two people who can never agree on anything." When she paused, he added, "The Dom Perignon is already chilling."

"Dom Perignon?" Her fingers clenched in her lap; she relaxed them. Why not? Jessica wondered. For once, work could wait. She laughed, suddenly and with delight. She was being irresponsible, and it felt wonderful. When she spoke, her tone was light, teasing. "Well, after all, I *do* have to eat."

"Uh-huh." Clay pulled out of the parking garage. "And why eat Happy Burgers when we can have gourmet?"

"Right." She shot him an amused glance. "And we *did* just sell two pretty tough customers."

"Oh yeah, the toughest."

"My desk is clear." She folded her arms across her chest, pushing away a nagging uneasiness. "It's not as if I have to punch a time clock." She fidgeted with the cuff of her blouse for a moment, then lifted her chin. "When we get to the restaurant, I'll just call the office and give Father the good news. After that the afternoon is ours."

As promised, Jessica called the office. Her father was out, but she left word with Barbara that the presentation had been a success. Lunch was an equal success—the food was delicious, the service impeccable, the atmosphere indulgent.

Then why couldn't she relax? Jessica asked herself, watching as the waiter cleared their dessert plates, then refilled their cups. She checked her watch; it was almost four. She pleated and repleated the edge of the lace tablecloth; she nervously sipped her coffee.

Clay glanced at her face, then lowered his eyes to her fidgeting fingers. "Jess, if it'll make you feel better, call in."

She jumped at the opening. "You're right. You're absolutely right. Something might have come up." She tossed her napkin onto the table and stood. "I'll be right back."

Jessica took two steps and stopped, swinging back toward Clay. "I'm being ridiculous, aren't I? I called Father, he knows the status of the account, he knows I won't be in this afternoon. I told Barbara where I was and she has the number." Jessica took a deep, steadying breath as she sat down again. "If they need me they'll find me."

"Congratulations," Clay murmured with a soft smile.

Her brow furrowed. "For what?"

"Never mind." He caught her hand across the table. "Tell me about your mother."

Jessica shrugged and looked away. "It's really not a big deal. Mother walked out on us when I was thirteen. I chose to stay with Father, Ali chose Mother."

Clay saw the cold creep into her eyes, felt her fingers stiffen under his. "You're still angry with her."

"Don't be silly. I'm an adult now, I can deal with it."

He squeezed her hand when she tried to draw it away. "Why did you choose to live with your father?"

"Why is this important?" Jessica countered.

"Because," he said softly, "to me everything about you is important."

Tears caught in her throat, she swallowed past them. "I was angry, hurt.... She walked out on us.... I couldn't desert him."

"Even when Ali did?" Clay asked.

"Yes..." She lowered her eyes, not wanting him to see that they were bright with tears. "That fed my anger. Not only had she left me—she'd taken Ali away as well. I was terribly lonely afterward. As I'm sure you can imagine, Bill wasn't a terribly demonstrative father."

"Oh, princess—"

"No, Clay—" she took a deep breath "—I'm on a roll now, don't stop me. I saw Mother several times at the beginning, but it was so uncomfortable for us both.'' Jessica's fingers tightened on his. ''Actually, I was as mean to her as a thirteen-year-old daughter knows how to be; I kept thinking that if I made her feel guilty enough she'd come back home. It didn't work, of course. She told me to call her when I wanted to see her. I never did.''

''Never?''

''I sent her a high school graduation announcement, birthday and Christmas cards, kept in touch by way of Ali, but...'' Her words trailed off, and silence fell over the table. After a moment she shook her head. ''I was wrong. I acted like a spoiled brat. As an adult I know that. But I haven't completely forgiven her for walking out. I can't Clay. I just can't.''

Clay's heart went out to her. She was sitting ramrod straight, shoulders squared, chin up. Although her voice was husky with emotion, her words quavered only slightly. She was the picture of control but for her eyes—they were brilliant with moisture, opaque with pain.

Many people would deny responsibility for their actions. Many would overdramatize the telling to elicit sympathy, and others wouldn't tell the whole truth. But not Jessica. She was proud without being blind, vulnerable without being a victim. Clay reached his other hand across the table to clasp hers. Their eyes met and held. ''So, we'll go to the opening; the peace will begin.''

''Let's go home,'' Jessica whispered, lifting his hands to her lips, placing a gentle kiss first on one, then the other. ''I need to hold you, make love to you.''

They stood and left the restaurant.

Eight

The rest of the week flew by in a flurry of creative meetings, laughter and lovemaking. Clay was a tireless and demanding lover, and by Sunday night Jessica couldn't push away the niggling guilt her changed life-style had created. Desperate to get a few extra hours of work in, she talked Clay into accompanying her to the office. As the elevator doors slid open, Clay pulled Jessica into his arms. "Aw, come on, Jess," he wheedled, nibbling at her neck, "it's Sunday."

Goose bumps raced over her flesh at the caress and Jessica groaned. Taking a deep breath, she stepped out of his arms. "Mr. Schneider doesn't care if it's Christmas. He wants this media buy tomorrow. It won't take long, I promise." She pushed the Open button, but as the doors responded, Clay reached around her and punched the Close button, then pulled her back into his arms. Her back was pressed against his chest, his warm breath stirred her hair. Jessica's pulse jumped.

Clay moved his hands from her waist to cup her breasts. "Ever do it in an elevator, princess?"

Oh, God... She squeezed her eyes shut. His voice held a trace of laughter, a hint of challenge, it was husky with desire...and she was incredibly aroused. "You're making this very difficult, Clay."

"Yeah, but then I'm a very bad boy."

She laughed but moved resolutely out of his arms. "Once I get started on this buy, it won't take long."

"All right, all right." He held up his hands in surrender. "I'm following you." The doors slid open once again and Jessica and Clay stepped into the dark reception area.

"Would you mind making coffee?" Jessica tossed the request over her shoulder as she flipped on the lights and headed into her office.

"Sure. Decaf?"

"Mmm, no...the real thing. Thanks." Jessica heard him mutter something and glanced up, already preoccupied with planning the media buy. "What?"

"Nothing." Clay shook his head and crossed to the door. "Get to work, I'll bring you a cup."

Minutes later, Clay found her behind her desk, surrounded by media kits from at least a dozen radio and television stations, her fingers flying over the keys of the adding machine. She didn't look up when he entered.

"Coffee, as you requested—strong, black, sure to keep the strongest of men awake." He set it on the desk with a flourish.

"Mmm...thanks." She gestured vaguely. "Put it anywhere."

Clay lifted his eyebrows in annoyance. "I'll just sit here and read a magazine. Don't let me bother you. Pretend I'm not here." He flopped into the chair across from her.

"Mmm...fine." After a moment, Jessica raised her eyes, then lowered them quickly. Why did he have to sit right in front of her? He was sprawled in the chair, one leg dangled provocatively over an arm, his jeans stretched tautly over his thighs and hips. How was she supposed to concentrate with that view?

"Don't let me disturb you," he repeated, picking up a journal and noisily flipping through it. "Pretend I'm not here."

"Mmm..." The magazine pages crackled as he turned them and Jessica groaned when she punched in an incorrect number for the third time. The dangling leg was now swinging rhythmically back and forth, back and forth.... He absently rubbed his thigh as he read. Jessica groaned again, took a determined sip of coffee and promised herself she would ignore him.

Just as she'd regained her train of thought, Clay sighed loudly and tossed aside the magazine. It landed on the floor with a flapping thwack. Jessica took a deep breath and returned to the column of figures. Four thirty-second spots at... Her head jerked up. He was tapping a rock and roll tune on his leg and humming under his breath. The pencil snapped between her fingers. "Clay!"

"What?" He looked up, the picture of innocence.

"That." She stared pointedly at his thrumming fingers.

"Oh, sorry," he murmured, not looking sorry at all. "Go back to work. I'll be quiet." He smiled. "Really."

As the minutes passed, Jessica was aware of only Clay. He paced and sighed, he rustled the papers on her desk, he flipped through every journal in her office. "That's it!" she exclaimed, tossing her pencil on the desk in frustration.

"Great, you're finished. Want to grab a pizza on the way home?"

What she would like to do was grab him by the throat and shake him silly, she thought, her gaze settling on the open collar of his shirt. Of course, gagging him, then tying him to a chair was another option. Or tickle torture. Or—

Clay shoved his hands into the back pockets of his jeans and grinned. Judging by the light in her eyes, he could imagine what was going on in her head. He almost laughed out loud; if he were a cautious man he would stop now. He wasn't. "You *are* finished, aren't you?"

"Finished?" Her voice was incredulous. "I've barely started!"

He made a clucking sound with his tongue. "We've been here over an hour."

Jessica muttered a string of four-letter words under her breath as she began stuffing the media kits into her briefcase. That accomplished, she glared up at him. "How could I work with all your humming and pacing and sighing? Honestly, you're worse than a ten-year-old!"

Clay laughed. "A ten-year-old?"

"Indeed. You're also—" Her words were cut off as Clay rounded the desk and tumbled her into his arms. The briefcase slipped from her fingers, as he flattened her breasts against his chest. Her eyes met his in surprise.

"Could it be you're annoyed at yourself rather than at me?"

"Certainly not!" She squirmed in his arms. "Why in the world?—"

"Perhaps you're annoyed because you were more interested in me and what I was doing than in those silly papers." His grin was cocky. "Or because you think I'm sexy as hell and you couldn't push me out of your mind. Or because for once you weren't 'all business.' Tsk, tsk, Ms. Mann, you're slipping."

Jessica's lips twitched. He was right—her inability to concentrate was only partly his fault. She lifted her chin in playful challenge. "Sexy as hell? Really, Clay. You practically had to set up loudspeakers to get me to notice you." She fluttered her lashes provocatively. "But delude yourself all you want—"

"Thank you, I will," Clay murmured, lowering his lips to hers. When he pulled away, her taste was still sweet against his lips. "May I delude myself again, Ms. Mann?"

"Please do," she whispered. His lips were warm. His touch was as gentle as a spring rain, as intoxicating as moonshine. She ran her hands up his back, winding her fingers into his hair and pulling him closer, wanting to drown in his taste and touch.

The buy was waiting; she didn't care. She could work all night. At this moment, all she knew, all she cared about was Clay. Her memory extended no farther than the moment he'd pulled her into his arms, her future consisted only of the touch of his flesh against hers. She knew a throbbing warmth, an aching sweetness. There was laughter in her voice as she asked, "Ever do it in a vice-president's office, barbarian?"

Clay's laughter answered her and they sank to the floor.

Gallery 3501 was one of the most prestigious and most chic galleries in Los Angeles. The owner, Salle Sweet, had a reputation for being bizarre—she teased her hair into a beehive, only wore clothes that were a shade of purple, and spoke with a fabricated accent. She also had a reputation for being shrewd—she took chances on relatively unknown artists and made them into stars.

Claire Mann was her most recent success, Jessica thought, gripping Clay's arm as they approached the gallery. The opening was so well-attended that the patrons spilled out of the doorway and into the street. *I'm not ready for this,* she repeated for the hundredth time since leaving the house. *I'm not in top form—I didn't get enough sleep and...* She didn't finish the thought, because she knew she was only making excuses. Tonight she would talk to her mother for the first time in years, and it scared the hell out of her.

"You look lovely," he murmured, hoping to reassure her.

Jessica glanced up at Clay. "You think so?" She smoothed an imaginary wrinkle in the pearl-gray silk and readjusted the single silver chain.

"Uh-huh." He lightly squeezed the hand gripping his arm. "Ready?"

Jessica paused briefly, then let Clay lead her through the crowd and inside. Her eyes flew over the room and she drew a sharp, surprised breath. Ali had said their mother was good—she wasn't good, she was great. Ali had said their mother did portraits—she didn't paint portraits, she portrayed people with an uncanny accuracy.

A painting across the room caught her eye. Jessica moved toward the life-size canvas—she had no choice, the painting demanded her attention—and stopped in front of it, tightening her fingers on Clay's arm. The painting had been done from a photograph; she recognized the shot as one Ali had taken last year. For one dizzying moment, Jessica felt as if she'd stepped into a carnival fun house, because staring back at her was herself.

"My God," Clay murmured, his eyes riveted on the portrait. It was simply titled *Jess,* and told him everything it'd taken him weeks to learn about her. Her stance was familiar—back straight, chin squared. Her expression was one he'd seen many times—the slight furrowing of the eyebrows, the unbendable determination, the dreamy eyes. The sun was brilliant behind her as a storm barreled in over the ocean. The painting was fraught with contradictions—it was as complicated and as fascinating as the woman herself.

Clay shifted his eyes from the painting to Jessica. She looked very young standing there, her cheeks wild with color, her eyes bright and vulnerable. The fingers at his elbow bit into his flesh, and Clay knew she was uncomfortable with such a personal and public portrayal.

"How do you like it?"

Jessica turned toward the lilting voice. Her mother was much as she remembered her. Still delicately beautiful, but with a sparkle and fire that gave her a presence a football player would envy. When she'd last seen her, the pale golden hair had been threaded with silver, but now it was the other way around. Jessica cleared her throat, unexpectedly touched by the vulnerability in the blue eyes. "I like it very much."

Clay broke the silence that stretched between them. "Ali's waving wildly at me. Perhaps I should go see what all the commotion's about before she begins jogging in place." He squeezed Jessica's hand lightly. "Excuse me."

Jessica clutched at his jacket for one panicked moment, then relaxed and released the fabric. She watched him cross the room, then turned to her mother, searching for something to say. When she spoke it sounded inane even to her own ears. "I don't remember you painting."

"No." Claire Mann paused. "Your father didn't like the smell of the paints; he hated the mess."

"Oh." That sounded just like him. But still . . . she lowered her eyes, then lifted them to meet her mother's. Jessica's were filled with accusation. "So you just gave up?"

Claire reached out to touch her daughter, then pulled her hand away without touching. "I gave up on your father, not on you, not on Ali."

Then why did I feel so abandoned? The words sprang onto her tongue, but Jessica swallowed them. "Did you even try? He loved you."

Claire made a sound that expressed something between humor and pain. "I tried, oh how I tried. I hope you never know the hurt and frustration I experienced year after year. As for love, your father—" She looked over her shoulder. Salle Sweet was calling her name, motioning for her to come and meet a small, balding man in a blue suit. "We need to talk, I want to try to explain how it was for me. Please . . ." This time she *did* grab Jessica's hands. "Call me. Promise you will."

"I don't know," Jessica murmured. Salle Sweet was heading determinedly toward them, and she felt trapped and pressured. "I have to think about it—"

"Promise me you'll call. Once, long ago, I left it up to you and you never did. I don't want to take that chance again." Claire's eyes and voice filled with tears.

Jessica's chest tightened as the words rushed past her lips. "I'll call next week. I promise."

"Thank you," Claire whispered, dropping Jessica's hands. "I must go."

Jessica watched her mother glide across the room, watched as she smoothed the gallery owner's ruffled feathers. Jessica realized her hands were trembling at the same moment that she found herself wanting to laugh. Feeling younger and more carefree than she had in years, she scanned the room for Clay. He was standing with Ali, but his eyes were on her. When she smiled, he grinned and gave the thumbs-up sign. Laughing and feeling lucky, she headed toward him.

The office was quiet, and the desk lamp cast an unnatural light over the otherwise dark room. Jessica readjusted her glasses and simultaneously took a sip of coffee. The drink was cold and she wrinkled her nose—how long ago had she poured it? She checked her watch and sighed. It was after seven.

Jessica tipped her head. What time had she promised Clay she would be home? Had she told him six-thirty or seven-thirty? Darn it, they'd argued over her decision to stay late at the office as it was. She tapped her pencil against the stack of papers in front of her. But there were too many distractions at home. A smile whispered across her lips. Clay was a constant distraction, yet one she couldn't refuse.

When the phone rang, Jessica grimaced; she must have told him six-thirty. "Jessica Mann."

"Jess, where are you? It's after seven."

"I'm at the office," she answered defensively. "Working."

Clay's voice softened. "I made spaghetti. The salad's tossed, the bread's buttered, the wine's breathing. Everything's here but you."

Jessica sighed. "I only have four more pages to proof, then I'm finished for the evening."

Clay was silent for a moment. When he spoke, his tone was low, frustrated. "I'm coordinating the entire creative package for Cookies from Heaven. Right now I've got three television storyboards hanging over my head because we begin shooting in twelve days. But at five I went home with the rest of the agency."

"It's only four pages—"

"Leave it. It's not on deadline."

"*I* like to be ahead of deadline," Jessica answered sharply.

There was a long silence; she regretted her words but knew she couldn't take them back.

"Do whatever you want, Jess. You know where to find me." With that, he hung up.

Jessica stared at the receiver in shock. He'd hung up on her! She couldn't believe it, he'd hung up on her. She slammed down the phone. The jerk, it wasn't her fault she had work to do! It wasn't her fault that he'd started dinner too early, or... Jessica shook her head, sank back into her chair and rubbed her temples. It *was* her fault, all of it. He was right—she wasn't on deadline. And he'd started dinner because she'd promised to be home by six-thirty—and now it was a quarter to eight. And he'd hung up on her because she deserved it.

Jessica's eyes filled, her cheeks grew warm. She wasn't being fair. She'd hurt him, and he'd been nothing but kind to her. Her arms suddenly ached to hold him; she was breathless with the need to apologize.

It's only four pages, she told herself, slipping the copy into her briefcase. *Take it home and do it while the pasta's cooking, or after dinner, or while Clay's sleeping. It's only four pages,* she repeated, switching off the light and heading for the elevator.

When Jessica got home, her condo was dark and unnaturally quiet. "Clay," she called out, softly closing the door behind her, "I'm home." There was no response and her heart began to beat a little faster.

"Clay," she called again, a little louder this time. "I'm home." Silence. *He's not here,* she thought, panic forming a hard knot in her chest. She swallowed past it, crossed to the couch, and switched on a light.

A novel lay open on the coffee table, there was a Snickers wrapper in the ashtray. Clay's favorite Nikes were stacked one on top of the other next to the couch. *He's not here,* she repeated, shoulders drooping. Pulling herself together, she squared her shoulders and headed slowly toward the kitchen. The light was on over the sink, evidence of a meal in progress was everywhere: the kettle of water on the stove, dishes and flatware out and ready, the half-empty bottle of wine on the counter.

Jessica crossed to the sink, staring out the window at the clear, black night. *He's gone. I've sent him away—*she caught her lower lip between her teeth—*I miss him.* Her fingers curled into fists. And all because of four stupid pages of copy.

"Jess?"

Jessica whirled around. He was standing in the doorway, shirt undone, hair tousled, feet bare. "You're here," she whispered, joy warming her cheeks.

"Where would you have me be?"

"Nowhere...I mean..." She lowered her eyes, her heart tap-dancing in her chest. "I called out, I thought...I thought you'd left me."

"I almost did."

"Oh." Jessica realized she was wringing her hands and shoved them into her pockets.

Clay gestured with his empty glass. "I came in for more wine." He brushed by her. "What are you doing home? I thought you had work to do."

Jessica stared for a moment at his stiff back, wishing he'd look at her. "I do, but I wanted...I needed to..." Her words trailed off.

"What, Jessica?" Clay swung around, pinning her with his angry gaze.

"I wanted to apologize."

"Fine. Consider it done." Instead of refilling his glass, Clay picked up the bottle. "Now, excuse me, you're cutting into my drinking time."

"Please don't go," Jessica whispered, catching his arm as he moved to pass her.

Clay shrugged off her hand. "Give me a reason to stay."

"Because I need you."

"Right now that's not good enough, Jess. Yesterday it would have been, maybe it will be again. But not now."

"What do you want me to say?" she asked in desperation. "I'm here, I've apologized.... I don't know what else to do!"

"I don't either. But I won't be second to your career. I can't play it that way." He turned and left the room.

Jessica watched him for one shocked moment, then raced after him. She caught his arm, and swung him around. "No...wait...I'm here because...you're more important than work."

"What did you say?"

She took a deep breath. "That you're more important than work."

A wicked smile lighted his face, and his eyes met hers. "Prove it."

At his smile, relief flooded through her. Crossing to him, she took the bottle and glass from his hands. "With pleasure."

Nine

At the end of two weeks, Jessica realized she'd come to depend on Clay. She depended on his smile in the morning, his tenderness at night. She depended on his understanding, his strength, his wacky approach to life.

Jessica sneaked a glance at him. They were curled up on the couch, watching a slapstick comedy Clay had rented. Or rather, Clay was watching. His laughter rumbled against her side, and she snuggled a little closer, resting her head against his shoulder.

Depending on him was scary. She'd never really needed anyone like this before. And who would think she, cautious, serious Jessica, would be leaning on someone as unpredictable and crazy as Clay? It defied all rational thought, but there she was, leaning on him.

Jessica smiled as Clay dropped a kiss on the top of her head. She was addicted to this crazy man, to his laughter, his warmth. The smile faded. But something had to give. Her father was sending more and more work her way, and she was scrambling to keep up. Just keeping up was a new experience; in the past she'd always been ahead of schedule, on top of things. No more. Her addiction to Clay was all-consuming. So the hours she used to devote to furthering her career, she now devoted to her addiction, and she felt a little bit out of control.

She sipped her wine, telling herself to enjoy it now because later, when Clay was asleep, it would be coffee, strong and black. Her father had asked her to review the entire package that the retail division had developed for the Shipson Furniture account and give him a report in the morning. It would take hours, and here she sat.

Clay heard her sigh and pulled his eyes from the antics of Curly, Larry and Mo, lowering them to her face and noting its contemplative look. "Something wrong, princess?"

She started guiltily. "What . . . no, just thinking."

"Oh no, not that," Clay said with a quick laugh. Twisting around, he pressed her back onto the couch. "My practical, serious Jessica, you get into trouble when you think too much." He smiled down at her flushed face. "I much prefer you this way."

"That," she murmured, her voice already husky with need, "was an extremely sexist remark."

"Uh-huh." Clay nibbled at the corners of her mouth. "What'cha gonna do about it?"

With a wicked laugh, she showed him.

Hours later Jessica lay very still, listening to Clay breathing, making sure he was asleep. She absolutely was *not* sneaking around, she assured herself. Nor did she think what she was doing was wrong. She just wasn't in the mood for an argument.

Cautiously she got out of bed, taking pains so that the mattress wouldn't spring back too quickly and jostle Clay. Tossing a last, lingering glance at the bed, she slipped into her robe and tiptoed out of the bedroom.

It's eleven o'clock now, Jessica thought, yawning as she entered the kitchen. She should be back in bed by two. The linoleum was cold against her bare feet and she propped one foot on top of the other while she made coffee, switching feet when the one on the bottom became numb. "Thank God for caffeine," she murmured, adding an extra scoop to the filter cup. While the coffee brewed, she set everything she would need at the kitchen table, then poured herself a cup and settled down to work.

Clay groaned and rolled over, automatically seeking Jessica's warm flesh. The other side of the bed was cool and Clay's lids fluttered up. No, it wasn't a dream, he was alone in the bed. He listened for a moment, then sat up, his eyes scanning the darkened room. No Jessica. Realizing this wasn't the first time he'd "dreamed" Jessica had left him in the night, he yawned, got out of bed and went to find her.

She was in the kitchen, surrounded by paperwork, sipping coffee from her favorite mug. She looked exhausted. "Jess, what're you doing up?" His voice was froggy with sleep.

Jessica started, sloshing coffee onto the report in front of her. "Damn it!" She quickly dabbed the liquid with the edge of her robe. Her annoyed eyes met his. "I'm working."

"It's three-thirty in the morning." He scratched his chest as he walked into the kitchen.

Her mouth slackened with surprise as her eyes darted to the clock. It was three-thirty and she was nowhere near done! A familiar tightness settled in her shoulders and neck, and her head began to ache.

"Come back to bed," he coaxed, stopping behind her and placing a kiss on top of her head. "I'm lonely without you."

Jessica squeezed her eyes shut. When she spoke, her tone was sharp with frustration and exhaustion. "I have to finish this by morning."

"What is it?" He peered over her shoulder.

"The Shipson Furniture package." She sighed. "I've got a ways to go, would you get me another cup of coffee?"

"Sure." He grabbed her cup and swung around to the pot. It was empty. Clay frowned. She consumed entirely too much caffeine and... His eyes narrowed as his head began to clear. He glanced back at her; something didn't add up. "Shipson...that's your father's pet project. What's he giving it to you for?"

Jessica made an annoyed sound. "I don't know. He dropped the whole thing in my lap late this afternoon. He wants me to evaluate the entire package."

"That doesn't make sense; he's been working with them all along. Don't you think his having you review his own work a little strange?"

Jessica's chin tilted. "Maybe he wants my opinion."

Clay snorted. "Bill?"

"Thanks a lot!" Jessica huffed, swinging back to the report.

"No, think about it, Jess." He waited until she met his eyes again. "Your father's been dumping a lot of work on you lately. Work with ridiculous deadlines even for advertising. If you ask me, most of it, including this, is busy-work."

"In my opinion," she returned furiously, "he's finally starting to trust me with his business. This shows he has confidence in my ability." When Clay snorted again, her cheeks flooded with color. "Go back to bed, I've got work to do."

"What you need to do," Clay said quietly, "is get some sleep. You look like hell."

"Just great!" She slammed her palm on the table as she jumped up and turned to face him. "Anything else you'd like to criticize?"

"Okay, fine." He jerked a hand through his hair in frustration. "You drink too much coffee. You keep unreasonable hours, you don't eat right."

Jessica made a choking sound. "This is rich! You're acting like the mother I didn't have."

His jaw tightened. "You have a mother, Jess. One you keep putting off. When are you going to see her?"

"What does my mother have to do with this blasted report?" She tossed her glasses onto the table.

He ignored her question. "How long has this been going on? I'd wondered why you were so tired, why there were circles under your eyes and you were losing weight." He rested his fists on his hips. "Well, Jessica? How long have you been lying to me?"

Jessica flushed. "I don't know what you're talking about! I haven't lied to you—"

"Maybe we should get a dictionary, because I think sneaking out of bed to work all night and never mentioning it is dishonest as hell."

"Why are you pressuring me?" She pushed back her hair. "I can't handle this right now; I don't have the time to deal—"

He grabbed her arms, turning her toward the window. "Look at yourself, Jess. You're falling apart."

"Well...it's just that...I..." Jessica shook her head helplessly when the words wouldn't come. Her shoulders drooped; she felt utterly defeated, utterly alone.

"Aw, princess." He gathered her into his arms and softly stroked her hair while she cried. "It's okay...I'm sorry."

Jessica rested against him, her tears dampening his robe, her fingers pressed over his steady heartbeat. "I'm so tired," she whispered. "So tired."

"I know, sweetie. I know." He massaged her back, relieved as her shuddered breathing evened.

"It's just that..." she curled her fingers into the soft terry cloth, keeping her face pressed against his chest "...it's just that, what I've worked so hard for is finally happening. I can't let him down. I can't lose his trust."

Clay bit back the things he wanted to say about her father, about the way she pushed herself. "How much do you have left to do tonight?"

"The creative rationale and the visuals." Her voice was heavy with fatigue.

"I'll help. Between the two of us, we can get it out in an hour."

"But—"

Clay pressed a finger to her lips. "I want to."

"Thank you," she whispered, pressing her cheek against his chest.

"I'm glad you talked me into joining you for lunch," Jessica said as she and Clay stepped off the elevator. "That soup really hit the spot."

"I'm glad, too," Clay murmured. He lifted his hand to touch her, then remembering his promise to behave only as her colleague when they were at the office, resisted the urge. With a small smile, he settled for a whiff of her perfume as they crossed the reception area together.

Not that they were fooling anyone, Clay thought, sneaking a glance at her as she absently smoothed her jacket. He suspected that everyone from her father to the cleaning staff knew what was going on. The smile widened; she would hate that.

Jessica motioned toward Barbara's desk. "I'm going to see if I have any messages." Her voice deepened as her eyes met his. "I'll catch you later."

"I look forward to it," Clay teased, wiggling his eyebrows. When her face heated, he stifled a laugh. Oh yeah, they were keeping some secret.

Jessica could feel Clay's eyes on her back as she crossed the room. She willed her face to cool, then silently swore when her flush increased at the receptionist's knowing glance. "Hi, Barbara. Any messages?"

The receptionist handed Jessica several, then took a deep breath. "Mr. Schneider was here."

Jessica's eyes lifted from the pink slips of paper. Barbara looked flustered. "Oh? Is there a problem?"

"He was furious. Your father ended up calming him down—"

"Wait a minute, Barbara." Jessica tucked the messages into her jacket pocket. "Why was he?—" Jessica paled. "Oh no, I'd scheduled a noon meeting to go over—"

"Bingo," Barbara interrupted. "He'd canceled another appointment and driven all the way across town in noon traffic. He was—"

"Furious," Jessica supplied, holding a hand to her forehead. She was appalled at having forgotten such an important meeting. "I'd better call him. Hopefully I can—"

"Jessica . . ."

Jessica glanced back over her shoulder; Barbara looked decidedly uneasy now. "Yes?"

"Your father wants to see you . . . immediately."

"Thank you, Barbara." Jessica's heart sank. Without pausing for thought, she headed for Clay's office.

He was at his drawing board and looked up when she entered. "You're not going to believe this," Jessica said, closing the door behind her.

"What's wrong?" He tossed the colored marker into a box filled with a hundred others and leaned back in his chair. "Somebody die?"

"Worse. I forgot I had a noon appointment with Rick Schneider. According to Barbara, he was livid."

"It happens all the time," Clay inserted quietly. "Don't get bent out of shape."

Jessica whirled on him. "It doesn't happen to *me* all the time. I consider it unforgivable and unprofessional to waste anyone's time like that."

"Call him, apologize, make excuses. It'll blow over."

"Father's already done that," Jessica moaned. "I'm supposed to go see him right away."

"Anything I can do?" Clay asked.

She stopped at the door, her eyes met his. "Wish me luck."

"Good luck," Clay murmured, watching her walk coolly, regally, toward the king's office.

Forty minutes later, Jessica carefully shut her father's door behind her and headed down the hall. It really wasn't fair, she fumed, still stinging from her father's reprimand. This was the first time—and only time, she promised herself—she'd ever missed an appointment, and she'd gotten caught. Her father absolutely never checked up on her, not when everything was going like clockwork, that is. But let one thing go wrong and there he was, waiting to pick her bones like a vulture.

Jessica flushed as she remembered not only his words, but his tone of voice—tight, disappointed, subtly condescending. He'd called her unprofessional, and insinuated that she wasn't concentrating on her career as much as her social life.

And she'd sat there and quietly taken it—without explanation or argument. After all, what could she have said? "You see, Father, I'm preoccupied with the affair I'm having with Clay." Or, "I missed my appointment because I'm so tired I can't see straight, let alone remember my appointments. You see, I stayed up all night to finish the Shipson report. Of course, I had time to watch a Three Stooges movie and go out for a pizza." Oh, that would have been great. Just great.

Jessica crossed her office, sinking into the chair behind her desk. She stared at Fred over steepled fingers. Even though she was in the wrong, it bothered her that he hadn't let this slide with just a word or two. Clay was right—appointments were missed all the time, it would blow over.

Besides, she'd never before performed under par, yet her father had acted as if she was a constant problem.

A frown wrinkled her brow. Weeks ago she'd sensed he was just waiting for her to make a mistake. She'd sensed that he wanted her off the cookie account, but had pushed her suspicions aside as unfounded. Now she wasn't so sure.

But why? Was he so uncomfortable having a woman as his second in command that he wanted to find concrete reasons to fire her? It was the only explanation she could think of. Fury and determination stiffened her spine. She would be damned if she would let him push her out! She'd worked too hard, had sacrificed too much to lose it all now.

Her eyes narrowed. Something had to give. She'd thought it before and had ignored the thought, not having liked her choices. She still didn't like the choices, but today's foul-up made changes a necessity.

The simple truth was that she'd forgotten her appointment because she was so tired she couldn't organize her thoughts, so rushed she couldn't catch her breath. Something had to go.

Not Clay. Oh, God, not Clay. The words rushed into her head, and she squeezed her eyes shut against the truth. He was the logical choice, but—

"Excuse me, Jessica?"

Jessica looked up to see Barbara standing in the doorway holding a floral arrangement. *Oh no, not again!* Jessica thought, knowing they were from Clay. If her father got wind of this... She eyed the arrangement for a moment. Clay had promised... Then she smiled. "Well, bring it here." Her smile widened as Barbara practically flew across the room.

Not flowers, Jessica realized as the other woman set it on her desk. Tootsie Pops. Her pulse fluttered, her cheeks warmed. He'd sent her a bouquet of lollipops. There were at least a dozen of them, all flavors, stuffed into a silly-looking ceramic pig. The gaudiest dyed-pink baby's breath was interspersed with the candy. The implications were endlessly uncomplimentary; she was delighted nevertheless.

"There's a card."

Jessica lifted her eyes, folding her arms across her chest. "I'm sure there is."

Barbara laughed. "If that's a hint that you want to be alone..." Her words trailed off as she sashayed toward the door, glancing over her shoulder when she reached it. "By the way, don't worry about this getting around. I've been bribed into silence."

As soon as she'd cleared the doorway, Jessica ripped open the envelope.

"I don't wear wing tips. Clay."

She brought the card to her lips and sagged against the chair. The man was crazy, and she was thoroughly charmed. All it had taken was a dime store pig, a bunch of suckers and a message whose meaning only a madman could decipher. The missed appointment, her father's stinging words, her fatigue, all dissipated before the warmth in her cheeks and heart.

She lovingly smoothed the card, then tucked it into her top desk drawer. She couldn't give Clay up; it wasn't even a choice. She would reorganize her time, delegate responsibility. She would stop taking unnecessary calls, only see suppliers whose services were immediately required, stop checking up on others' work.

Jessica plucked a grape lollipop from the bunch and popped it into her mouth. It would be okay, she assured herself as the sweet, distinctive flavor flowed over her tongue. Everything would be fine, there was more than enough time for Clay and her career.

If the last ten days had proved anything, it had been the fact that she'd lied to herself—there wasn't enough time for both Clay and her career. Jessica slipped out of her jacket

and hung it on the coat tree. She crossed to the window and
stared down at the street. It seemed years since she'd wanted
to enjoy the early morning light or the hours before deadline craziness set in. In fact, most mornings it was all she
could do to drag herself out of bed to make it to work by
nine. This morning she hadn't been so lucky—it was already after ten.

Frowning, Jessica turned away from the window. She'd
been up half the night again, working on another of her father's silly projects. The frown deepened at her choice of
adjective; reviewing one hundred and twelve résumés by this
morning wasn't silly, it was...busywork. She pushed the
description away. That was Clay's opinion, not hers. After
all, they had one art director's position open and they
wanted to find the most qualified individual for the job. But
until yesterday there hadn't been a rush, that is, not until her
father had dropped the ball into her lap at four-forty-two in
the afternoon.

Jessica sank into the chair behind her desk. Resting her
head against the back, her eyes fluttered shut. She was so
tired....

"Glad you could make it in this morning, Jessica."

Her eyes snapped open. Her father was standing in the
doorway, his expression even blacker than his tone. Jessica
leaned forward in her chair, calmly folding her hands in
front of her. "Bill." She lifted a brow. "Is there a problem?"

He strode across the room, stopping directly in front of
her. His eyes met hers; he tossed the latest issue of *California* magazine onto the desk. "Judge for yourself."

Jessica's eyes fell to the magazine. The back cover was a
full-page, full-color ad for New Age Clothing. "The pre-
view copy," Jessica murmured, her eyes racing over it,
mentally checking off the job specifications and matching
them to the ad. His and hers jumpsuits, high-top sneakers,
an outdoor shot, layout approved by client—she'd seen to

that herself—good quality photograph, address correct . . .
She came up with nothing out of line and lifted her eyes to
her father's. "It's a beautiful ad, I'm sure—"

Bill Mann placed his fists on the desk and leaned toward
her. "And how much did this 'beautiful ad' cost?"

Jessica's heart began hammering against her chest.
Something was very wrong. When her father talked money,
it was serious. She tipped her head in thought. "Production and media, about twenty-eight thousand dollars."

"Twenty-seven thousand, five hundred fifty-four, to be
exact." His eyes bored into hers. "That would be quite an
amount for the agency to eat, should there be a mistake."

Suddenly annoyed with his game of cat and mouse, Jessica stood and faced him. "There's obviously something
wrong with this ad, and since I don't know what it is, why
don't you clue me in?"

"All right, Jessica—" he tapped the ad for emphasis
"—every one of those prices is wrong."

Jessica paled. "That can't be." With one hand she
grabbed the magazine, with the other she pulled the New
Age file.

"Don't bother. Those figures—" he gestured in her
direction, "—aren't even in the ballpark."

Her eyes went from one column of figures to the other,
heart sinking. "Has the client seen?—" She never finished
the question; her father's face told her they had. "I can't
imagine how this happened. These figures are so far-off as
to be laughable."

"Why didn't you proof this before it went to the magazine? You should know better than not to double-check
prices on a national ad." His voice exuded disappointment. "What were you thinking of, Jessica?"

She lifted her chin. "For the salary we pay Jason, I assumed he could do his job. It's unproductive for me to check
up on everyone's—"

"So, you assumed this information was correct?"

Jessica flushed. "I didn't assume—"

"The clients have refused to pay for the ad. How do you propose I recoup a twenty-eight-thousand-dollar-loss?"

Jessica shoved her hands into her pockets, desperately clinging to her composure. "I'll talk to Jason right away. I'll find out where he got this information. There has to be a logical explanation."

"As far as I'm concerned," her father said, turning and walking to the door, "I've already gotten to the bottom of it." When he reached the door, he stopped, swinging around to face her. "That's two times in less than two weeks. I hired you because I thought you were a serious professional. I thought you were capable of running my business." His expression was suddenly sad. "Don't let me down again, Jessica." He turned again and left the room.

She watched him go, tears burning her eyes, her lungs near bursting from holding back a cry of pain and disappointment. She'd had it all and had lost it. Everything she'd worked for had been shot to hell by a jumble of numbers. Pressing a hand to her mouth, she stared at the empty doorway.

She was still staring when she arrived home that evening. This time at a sunset whose breathtaking beauty she didn't have the energy—or the heart—to enjoy. She wondered if she ever would again. At breaking point, she took a deep breath and stepped from the car.

She hadn't seen Clay all day, nor would she see him this evening—he'd been tied up at the Cookies from Heaven shoot. Jessica sighed as she unlocked the door. It was just as well, really. The phone rang just as she deposited her purse and briefcase on the couch. "Oh, shut up," she muttered, ignoring its jangle and heading toward the kitchen. Five, six, seven... Groaning, she retraced her steps.

"Hello."

"Hey, Jess. Just walking in?"

"Yes." Propping the phone between her neck and shoulder, she bent to unbuckle her shoes. "How's the shoot going?"

"We're finished. And it went great, just great! The weather and lighting were perfect." Clay's tone was as exuberant as a schoolboy's who'd just discovered girls. "Ben and Rita were the choice of a lifetime, they played their parts to a tee. I've already decided to use them in the bedroom commercial. We've got ourselves an award winner, Jess, I know it."

"I'm glad," Jessica murmured automatically.

"I thought you'd be thrilled." Clay's tone was suddenly quizzical. "Is something wrong?"

"Wrong? What could possibly be wrong?" Jessica drew her eyebrows together as she tried to force some life into her voice. "After all, you said we had an award winner." God, he was right, she should be glad—should be ecstatic—but she felt nothing but a numbing despair.

"I've got to hand it to you, Jess, the whole concept was a stroke of genius. It was the first time I've seen perfect harmony between brother and sister Miller."

"Oh...right...good," Jessica stuttered, jerking her eyes from a point on the far wall, not having the vaguest idea what he'd said.

"Jess, are you sure?—" He changed tack. "So, how was your day?"

She tightened her fingers around the phone cord. "Okay, really. What are you doing tonight? Is everyone going out?"

"Yeah, the cast and crew are meeting at Molly's.... But maybe I should come back to L.A. You sound—"

"Nonsense," Jessica interrupted crisply. "I'm going to eat a light supper and go to bed. Trust me, I'd be rotten company tonight."

"If you're sure..." Obviously unconvinced, his voice trailed away.

"Of course I'm sure. Go, have fun and let me get some rest. I'll talk to you in the morning." Without giving him time for more than a two-syllable farewell, she hung up.

Jessica stared at the phone for a moment, wishing he would call back, and at the same time praying he wouldn't. A confusing mixture of emotions rushed through her. She wanted to be alone; she wanted him with her. She was jealous of everyone he'd talk to tonight; she was well rid of him for the evening. With a last look at the silent phone, she turned and walked to the kitchen.

True to her words, Jessica busied herself in the kitchen, preparing a simple meal of eggs and toast. But when she sat down to eat, the food tasted like cardboard and she pushed it away in disgust. Too early for sleep, she tried reading, television, doing her nails. Nothing took her mind off her father's angry words. Finally she poured a glass of wine and paced. Four glasses and two hours later, she tumbled into bed, falling into a troubled sleep.

It was the black of dreams—the black your eyes never adjusted to, the kind of black that swallowed you whole. Someone was pounding on the door. They were insistent, beating faster, harder, until the door bowed with each blow. As the noise became unbearable, Jessica's eyes snapped open, then circled the darkened room in confusion.

Not a dream . . . not the door . . .

She clutched at the sheet with clammy fingers. She was flat on her back, pulse racing, heart slamming against her chest. Oh, God, Oh, God . . . What was wrong? My heart— I can't breathe, I'm going to die— As the wild thoughts ran through her brain, her heart increased its pace until the thudding in her head sounded like frenzied drums, until she thought her chest would give under the force of the blows.

Relax, Jessica told herself. *That's right, relax your entire body. Toes first, fingers, yes, that's it, clear your mind. . . .* She cautiously lifted her hand, pressing her fingers over the pulse point in her neck. *That's right, calm, even breathing...relax....*

Just as her pulse began to slow, just as sweet relief was within reach, her heart sped back up, and she cried out in a combination of frustration and fear.

The bedroom door opened and her wide, frightened eyes flew to the patch of light and shadowy figure; the whimpering in her throat sounded more animal than human.

"Jess. My God, what's wrong?"

"Clay...my heart's p-pounding. I ca-can't breathe."

Her breath was coming in short, quick bursts and Clay dropped the motorcycle helmet and backpack and ran to the kitchen, returning in a moment with a paper bag. He held it to her lips. "Breathe into this. Good, just like that. You're going to be fine," he murmured reassuringly, watching as the paper bag expanded and contracted. "It's okay, sweetheart, everything will be all right." When her breathing had evened, he took away the bag.

Jessica grabbed his hand. "Clay, I...I'm...scared. My heart's still—"

"Shh...relax." He brushed the sweat-soaked hair from her forehead; her flesh was cold and damp against his fingers. "You're having an anxiety attack. But you're not going to die. Just try to relax." He continued to stroke her forehead. "All you can do is ride it out. Empty your mind of fear, close your eyes and relax."

Jessica did as he said and within moments her heart had slowed and a sweet lethargy began to take over her limbs. Her lids fluttered back up. "Why are you here?" she whispered. "I thought—"

He ran a gentle finger down her nose. "I went to dinner, but you sounded so strange on the phone, I had to make sure you were okay."

Jessica pulled herself into a sitting position, a frown marring her brow. "Just now, how did you know what was happening to me?"

"Personal experience," Clay murmured.

"Oh." Unable to meet his eyes, she nervously plucked at the bedspread. "You don't seem like an anxiety kind of guy."

"Not anymore, I'm not." A smile tugged at the corners of his lips. "Can I get you anything?"

She still didn't meet his eyes, but continued to toy with the bedspread. "No. I . . . Clay, this has never happened to me before."

"I know." He took her hand. "An anxiety attack is your body's way of telling you to take it easy."

"Yes," she whispered, coming to a painful decision. Taking a deep breath, she lifted her eyes. "Yes, I've been doing too much, I need to simplify." Pushing aside the covers, she cautiously got out of bed.

"Jess?" Clay frowned as he watched her slip into her robe and slippers, then cross the room to stare thoughtfully out the window. "What happened today?"

She swung around, clasping her hands in front of her. "Clay, we need to talk about us. I mean, I've never had a relationship like this before and I don't know if . . . I don't have . . ." Jessica shook her head, frustrated that the words wouldn't come. She, who was usually eloquent and persuasive, was fumbling like an adolescent in an unfamiliar social situation.

Taking a deep breath, she forced the words past her lips. "Today Father pointed out that I made a twenty-eight-thousand-dollar mistake. And while he was at it, he insinuated that if I disappointed him again, he'd fire me. And speaking of being fired, this afternoon I fired Jason French. Even though he deserved worse, firing a man who has a family to support isn't the most pleasant experience."

"I take it Jason was somehow at the root of the twenty-eight-thousand-dollar mistake."

She balled her hands into fists, and her gaze swung back to Clay. "Do you know what he did? He didn't know the prices of the merchandise in the New Age ad...so he guessed. An account executive taking home fifty grand a year made up the prices for a national ad. He was too lazy to even walk down the hall and ask me. I wanted to strangle him."

"I don't blame you," Clay murmured, standing and moving toward her. "I'd have wanted to kill him, and I'd have fired him. What does this have to do with us?"

She lifted her chin; her gaze met his. "I've been scrambling to keep up with my increased work load. When I forgot my appointment with Rick Schneider, I realized I didn't have enough time to do everything, so I made the decision to cut any unnecessary responsibilities. One of those was checking up on other people's work." She paused. "That decision cost the agency twenty-eight-thousand dollars." Her voice deepened. "It cost me my father's respect."

"Jess, you made a sound decision. Top account execs, like Jason French, don't need to be checked up on. What happened was a fluke."

"Right," she muttered sarcastically. "Fluke or not, I dropped the ball. If I hadn't been so rushed—"

"That's your father's guilt trip," Clay said angrily. "And as far as I'm concerned, this has nothing to do with us."

"Nothing to do with us?" Jessica dragged both hands through her hair, her tone incredulous. "It has *everything* to do with us. The only reason I'm scrambling at work is because we spend so much time together! I streamlined other responsibilities when I knew I should cut down my time with you."

"I don't believe this," Clay said, a muscle jumping in his jaw. "With all the garbage in your life, you're going to simplify it by giving me the heave-ho?"

"There are only so many hours in the day and I still want to see you, but—"

"But this relationship is too intense," he improvised. "I need some time, some space."

"What's wrong with that?"

In two steps he was upon her, holding her upper arms in a tight grip. "I don't operate that way, princess. It's one way with me—intense and totally involved. I won't settle for less."

"What are you saying? All or nothing?" Her hands were trembling as she pushed him away. "How can you do that to me? You know how much my career means to me! How can you demand so much of my time?" Her eyes filled with tears and she turned away from him. "I want to continue seeing you and I want to be with you, but I can't throw away my shot at the big time."

She swung back, suddenly furious. "I've given up everything for my career! Everything! Now you stand there and ask me to sacrifice it all. You're not playing fair, Clay."

"Are you playing fair? You want to call all the shots. You want to tell me when, where and for how long we can be together. That stinks, Jessica."

His tone grew gentle. "I'm not asking you to give everything up, Jess. You're good at what you do, and you love doing it. It's an important part of who you are, and I'd never ask you to throw it away. But I am asking you to be reasonable about the amount of work you do, about the amount of time you put into it. Maybe nine to five isn't enough, but nine to nine is too much. There's more to life than paperwork and meetings."

"And what am I supposed to tell my father when he hands me a report at four o'clock in the afternoon? Sorry, Bill, I've checked out for the evening?"

"Exactly. I still say he's putting you through some sick endurance test—"

"What do you know about my father?" Jessica cried. "What do you know about responsibility, about commitment? You do a job, then waltz off to some godforsaken place to play. Who do you think stays and runs the show? Who do you think keeps the agency going? Me!" Her voice rose. "How dare you talk to me about simplifying, how dare you suggest my father—"

He grabbed her arms again, forcing her to look at him. His jaw was clenched so tightly that his words sounded as if they were being forced through his teeth. "For eight years I played your game, Jessica. For eight years I put my career before everything else. Including my health." He shook her, only slightly. "I was smoking two and a half packs of cigarettes a day, my blood pressure was up to one hundred-seventy over one hundred, I had to anesthetize myself with liquor to get to sleep at night. I even managed to ignore the anxiety attacks. But I was the best, Jessica." He laughed without humor. "The best basket case, the best candidate for a heart attack. My last year in the fast track I won fourteen Clios, including creative director of the year, but I realized they wouldn't keep me alive...and they weren't making me happy. I saved myself, Jessica."

Until he uttered those last words she'd been surprised by his story, even touched. But now she was angry. Shaking off his hands, she stepped away from him. "So now you want to save me. Well, I don't need saving, Lancelot. I have no problem handling pressure, or didn't until you came along, that is."

"That's bull. You were scrambling to keep up before you met me." When she started to protest, he added, "Having nothing in your life but work is scrambling, Jessica. A career is supposed to be a part of your life—not all of it."

"That's your opinion, Clay. People in high-powered, high-paying positions have to put in more time and more sweat than other people. That's reality. Do you think Lee Iacocca checks out at five every evening, or that Leona Helmsley says goodbye to the office for the weekend? I think not."

"Is that really what you want from your life, Jessica?" His eyes bored into hers. "If it is, you'll end up just like your father."

Jessica tilted her chin. "And what's wrong with that? My father owns a multi-million-dollar agency, is a respected professional and—"

"And what, Jess? Does he have a loving family and a good home life? Or lots of friends and a busy social calendar? Does he date or take fabulous trips?"

Jessica's mouth snapped shut. She squared her shoulders. "My father has nothing to do with my ability to handle pressure."

"No—" his voice softened "—but he has to do with you, and consequently with us." Reaching out, cupping her face in his palms. "So tell me, princess, are we totally involved, or are we nothing?"

"Couldn't we try it my way, Clay?" she coaxed. "Just for a while?" She squeezed his hand. "You've been happy at the agency; you could stay."

He slipped his fingers from hers. "You don't get it, do you? You haven't heard one word I've said. I won't go back to that life, Jessica. Not for you, not for anybody."

Jessica felt as if he'd kicked her squarely in the chest. He was serious about this—it wasn't fair! Her tone was low but fierce as she said, "Don't make me choose, Clay."

"If you have to choose," Clay murmured, dropping his hands and stepping away, "then there's really no choice at all." Without another glance, he stooped to retrieve his backpack and helmet, then walked to the door.

Don't go! The plea from another night, another moment between them sprang to her lips; she didn't utter it. She held in the words and the tears, and feeling more alone than she ever had, Jessica watched him walk out of her life.

Ten

"Good morning, Clay." Jessica's smile was stiff, her complexion pasty.

"Good morning, Jessica."

He nodded coolly and stepped around her. Jessica's posture was rigid as she continued down the corridor to her office. Once inside, door closed behind her, her shoulders drooped, her chin sagged. It'd been a week since the night she'd let him go, and in that time the only words they'd exchanged were formal greetings like the one of a moment ago.

She still couldn't believe he was serious about forcing her to choose between him and her career. It wasn't fair. Jessica sank into her chair, dropping her head into her hands. It didn't make any sense, his claim that if she had to choose, there was no choice at all. Of course there was a choice! Life was full of them!

Lifting her chin, Jessica glared at Fred, swimming complacently around his bowl. Hadn't Clay ever heard of compromise? Of juggling schedules, of give and take? He was selfish and arrogant and unrealistic.

Jessica sighed. Rationalizing that everything was Clay's fault wasn't helping her state of mind—she was going crazy, anyway. She couldn't concentrate on work, vacillated between chocolate binges and being unable to eat at all, and wondered if she would ever sleep again. The simple truth was, she missed him.

Jessica squared her shoulders and straightened her spine. She would get over Clay. She had her career, the life she'd always known and enjoyed. It wasn't as if she were in love with the man. The thought brought a strange fluttering sensation to her chest.

It was time to put the past months behind her, forge ahead with her career plans. Resolutely she pulled out the Schneider file, slid open her top desk drawer in search of a pen. Her fingers rested for a moment on the card she'd stuck there weeks before. "I don't wear wing tips." The words rushed into her head and Jessica ignored the sudden urge to weep, telling herself it was just the melancholy time of her cycle. She pushed the card to the back of the drawer, pulled out a pen and opened the file.

"Jessica, do you have a moment?"

She looked up; Clay was standing in the doorway holding a mechanical. Hope surged through her until she thought she would burst with it; her palms began to sweat. "Of course."

"I have the ad that's running Sunday for you to okay." He handed it to her, then crossed to the window.

Of their own accord, her eyes strayed from the ad to Clay's stiff back. Her gaze lingered there, and she willed him to turn around and look at her. He didn't, and disappointment left a bitter taste in her mouth. Her eyes returned to the mechanical in front of her.

"So?"

She tightened her fingers on the mechanical at the curtness of his tone. She met his gaze coolly. "It looks fine. If the client has approved the layout, send it to the publication."

"No problem." He took the artwork from her hands and without another word, left the office.

Jessica was left with an incredible craving for chocolate.

"Barbara, I need you to make a reservation at Gregory's for noon Wednesday. There'll be two of us."

At Clay's words, Jessica's hand jerked and the just-poured coffee sloshed over the rim of the cup, nearly splattering her skirt. She took a deep, steadying breath, telling herself she didn't care who he was having lunch with...and she certainly wasn't jealous. Squaring her shoulders and pasting on a cool smile, she crossed to him.

"Clay, I talked to Sandra Miller this morning."

"Oh?"

Clay glanced at her, his expression annoyingly neutral. It was almost as if he were looking right through her, and Jessica swallowed past the lump that had formed in her throat. "Yes, she and Ty are a little concerned about the site chosen for the third commercial. Apparently they feel the location is a little remote."

"I'll take care of it immediately...Jessica."

The subtle stress he placed on her full name hurt. The hurt trembled on her nerve endings and she prayed it didn't show in her eyes. Working to maintain her calm, she arched a delicate eyebrow, then tipped her head imperiously. "See that you do." She saw the quick flash of anger, and satisfaction tilted the edges of her mouth. This time, she walked away from him.

* * *

Six days later, Clay headed for Bill Mann's office. It was time to get on with his life, he thought, slanting a glance into Jessica's office as he passed. The cookie campaign was finished, and so was the relationship.

Jessica was obviously happy; she seemed to be performing at peak efficiency. He'd even heard through the office grapevine that she'd been out with Mr. Wingtips. And when he'd heard, he'd wanted to throttle that stodgy old geezer, then find Jessica, drag her to his bed and make love to her until she was too sated to argue with him.

He could imagine Jess's fury at being slung over his shoulder and carried from the office, and he could imagine himself doing it. The corners of his lips lifted in a sardonic grin. The princess and the barbarian; some things never changed.

Clay shoved his fists into his pockets. Now all he had to do was convince himself that Jessica wasn't soft or vulnerable or a romantic, convince himself she was what he'd first thought—an ice princess, a business barracuda.

Sure, no problem, Clay thought with bravado. She was cold and bossy and he was better off without her. Furious that he still didn't believe himself, he knocked on Bill Mann's open door.

"Bill, could I see you for a moment?" Clay didn't wait for an answer, but instead, strode boldly into the room.

The older man looked up from the papers in front of him, his smile immediate but cool. "Have a seat, Clay."

"I prefer to stand." Clay's voice was gruff and he cleared his throat. Afraid of what he might say if he looked Bill Mann in the eye, he wandered to the window and stared out at the smoggy day.

"What's on your mind, Clay?"

Clay glanced over his shoulder, then turned back to the window. "My work on the cookie account is almost complete. Jessica and I just reviewed the dubs of the first Cookies from Heaven commercial." And she wouldn't even look at me, Clay silently added. We treated each other like strangers *instead of the lovers we are.* Lovers we were, he corrected. *And you're partly to blame.*

Clay swung around to face Jessica's father, anger and animosity rising like bile in his throat. "The commercial is fabulous, by the way."

"I knew it would be," Bill said, leaning back into the oversize chair and lighting a cigarette. He watched the smoke curl lazily toward the ceiling. After a moment, he added, "That's why I keep calling you, Clay. You're the best."

"Jessica's the best," Clay shot back. "The final concept was hers, not mine."

Bill Mann's eyes narrowed. "What did you want to see me about? Another assignment?"

"No." Clay moved back to the window. "I'm leaving."

"Is that so?"

"Yes. I don't know when I'll be back."

"Where's it going to be this time, Clay? Wisconsin again? The Bahamas?"

There was a smugness in Bill Mann's tone and Clay shot him a sharp look. The man looked as content as a tomcat surveying a hurt bird, and this time it was Clay's eyes that narrowed. "I can see my news has pleased you."

Bill's expression cleared. "No, of course not. We'll miss your expertise. In fact, I was ready to offer you another account, but now..."

But now you have exactly what you want, Clay silently finished, his eyes never leaving the older man's. You old bastard, you wanted me out of the picture, *and now you're so delighted you're almost squirming in your seat.*

Bill coughed. "So, my boy, when are you leaving?"

Clay stared at him for a moment, then said, "I have some loose ends to tie up, but I promise you'll be the first to know when."

Her mother had picked a neighborhood restaurant, really no better than a greasy spoon. A smile touched Jessica's lips as she imagined her father's face if she'd suggested dining here. *At least it's clean,* Jessica thought, glancing around the small café.

"Afternoon. You waiting for someone?" the waitress asked, expertly snapping her gum.

"Yes." Jessica cleared her throat, twisting her hands nervously in her lap. "I'm meeting my mother."

"Okay, darlin', you just let me know when you're ready."

"Of course," Jessica murmured, watching her hurry toward the kitchen. She checked her watch. Her mother was late; Jessica wondered if that was customary for her. She also wondered if she frequented this place. Her second question was answered as her mother rushed in, calling a familiar greeting to the waitress as she did so.

"Sorry I'm late." Her mother slid into the booth. "I have a problem with schedules."

"So does Ali," Jessica murmured. Another question answered, she thought quickly, her eyes racing over her mother. She'd been painting. There was a turquoise smudge on her right cheek, and her oversize denim shirt was splattered with paint.

"Claire, this is your little girl?" The waitress paused to snap her gum again. "I didn't know you had two daughters. How come I've never met this one before?"

There was a moment of uncomfortable silence before Claire said, "Jessica just moved back from New York."

"You don't say. Good to meet you, Jessica. I'm Mavis." When Jessica smiled in greeting, she continued, "Have the usual, Claire?"

"Yes." Then, by way of explanation, Claire turned to Jessica and said, "A California omelet—avocado, cheddar cheese and onion, topped with sour cream and sprouts. It's very good."

"That'll be fine," Jessica said, handing her menu to the waitress. "And coffee."

Once they were alone, Jessica lowered her eyes and trailed her finger along the vinyl tablecloth. What should she say? Commenting on the weather or inquiring about her health seemed so painfully superficial. Her mother was obviously experiencing the same loss for words because the moment of awkward silence stretched into many.

Her mother broke the silence first. "Are you still seeing the man I met at the opening? He was very nice. And very handsome."

"No." Jessica dropped her hands to her lap and looked away.

"I'm sorry. Of all the questions to break the ice with. I only asked because...you were so obviously in love...." Claire's words trailed off.

"I wasn't in love with Clay," Jessica said, clenching her fingers in her lap.

"Oh?" Claire Mann's eyebrows rose.

"We were just friends." She grimaced. That sounded ludicrous even to her own ears, and tried again. "Good friends, that is. Colleagues and..." This time it was her voice that trailed away.

"I was so sure—"

"I thought we were meeting to talk about you," Jessica interrupted.

Claire flushed. "Yes, of course." She fell silent as Mavis approached with their omelets. When they were once again alone, she said, "I've always wanted to try and explain to you how it was with your father and me."

"Why?" Jessica asked, suddenly defensive. "I didn't matter when I was thirteen. Why now?" Tears flooded her mother's eyes and Jessica felt remorse. She lightly touched her mother's hand. "I'm sorry. That was—"

"No, don't apologize. We need to be honest with each other. You're still angry and hurt, for years you...hated me." Claire lifted the coffee cup to her lips, then lowered it without sipping. "And I'm going to be honest with you. Life with your father was hell. He was cold and unapproachable; his career always came first."

"He loved you," Jessica insisted. "I know he did."

"That depends on how you define love. I was convenient. I took care of you and Ali, I kept his house, I was a good hostess. He disapproved of my friends and my painting; the only time we ever went out was when he needed me to entertain a business associate's wife."

"Then why did you marry him?" Jessica demanded, her cheeks hot with color.

"Because I confused being intrigued with being in love. He was different from every other man I'd ever known or dated. He was intense, brooding. It wasn't until after we were married and you were on the way that I realized my mistake. You see, he was obsessed with his career. That was all he talked about; every step he took was designed to move him up the ladder." Claire squeezed her hand into a fist. "I could have put up with most of it for your and Ali's sakes if only he'd talked to me or given me some emotional support." She lowered her voice. "If only he'd treated me like a human being."

Jessica's face drained of color. "So you left."

"Yes, I had no other choice. He said he wouldn't give me a divorce, wouldn't leave his own home. He made it clear that I'd have to leave if I wanted out, and told me I'd get nothing. At that time there weren't nearly as many divorces, and I'd never even heard the term mental cruelty. I believed he had all the power.'' There was a long pause. ''I left with nothing but my clothes . . . and Ali.''

Jessica lifted her chin. ''If he was as bad as you say, how could you have left me with him? What kind of mother would do that? Apparently I didn't mean as much to you as your freedom.'' Jessica heard her mother's quick intake of breath, but felt no satisfaction at having hurt her. She looked away.

Claire's voice trembled as she said, ''Easy? You call a decision that has haunted me day and night for seventeen years easy?'' She took a sip of water to steady herself. ''At thirteen you could choose the parent you wanted to live with. Your father knew that and used you as a weapon to hurt me. He was successful in that—I've never stopped hurting over losing you.''

Jessica's gaze snapped up, fury curling through her. ''You're telling me he never wanted me at all! He's all I had; how can you say that to me?''

''That's not what I'm saying! You were always more your father's child than mine—cautious, serious and meticulous. And you tried so hard to please him. You thought the sun rose and set on his shoulders. He knew that as well as I; he knew you'd choose him.''

After a moment, Claire continued. ''I was devastated when you chose to stay with him, but not surprised. I wasn't totally surprised by your anger either, because of the way you doted on him. But I had to save myself, Jess. I couldn't live that way, and as much as I pleaded, there was no way to convince him that there was more to life than work.'' She grabbed Jessica's hand, squeezing tightly. ''I've never stopped loving you, Jessica. Never stopped thinking about you and wishing you'd forgive me.''

Tears caught in Jessica's throat; she gulped past them. Her chest was tight, as if a brick had lodged there, and she struggled to breathe evenly. But worse than the physical discomfort was the utter confusion. Everything she'd thought a given was being challenged, everything she'd thought a truth was being questioned. Words and emotions raced around her head, creating a confusing mixture of revelation, pain and denial.

"I've got to go," Jessica whispered, her voice hoarse with emotion.

"No... please stay and talk to me!" Claire tightened her fingers on Jessica's.

"I can't." Jessica's voice cracked and she tried to clear her throat. "I need to think." She pulled her hand from her mother's, stood and fled the restaurant.

It seemed to Jessica days rather than hours since she'd left her mother in the restaurant. The sun dipped low in the sky, nature's sounds and colors had shifted subtly from midday brassy to late afternoon violet.

She scooped up some sand, letting it sift slowly through her fingers. It couldn't be true; she knew in her heart it was. So much hurt, so much waste. For years she'd thought her mother the villain. She should have realized that in life there were no villains, only losers.

Jessica stood and brushed the sand off the seat of her linen slacks, then stooped to retrieve her shoes. Sand had worked its way into her stockings, her hair had freed itself from its restraints and tumbled around her shoulders. She didn't care.

Jessica frowned at the sinking sun, knowing she had to get back to the office but not really giving a damn. She'd been sitting on the beach ever since she'd left her mother, thinking, trying to separate truth from fiction, the objective from the subjective. She hadn't found any answers, or any peace of mind.

She walked slowly down the beach in the direction of her car, knowing she was going into the office more from habit than because she wanted to. She laughed out loud. It was ironic—she'd lost Clay because she worked too hard, and now she had no desire to work at all. Shaking her head, she unlocked the car door, slipped inside and headed downtown.

When Jessica stepped off the elevator, Barbara looked up aghast. "My God! Jessica, where have you been?"

Jessica lifted her head and looked at Barbara in surprise. "The beach," she answered, turning toward her office.

Barbara's eyes widened. "Wait.... Don't you want your messages?"

"What? Oh, of course." Jessica shook her head as if to clear it and crossed to the receptionist's desk. She didn't even look at the handful of pink slips, just stuffed them into her pocket.

"Are you all right, Jessica? I mean..." Barbara's voice trailed away as her eyes swept over Jessica's rumpled clothes, wild hair and blank expression.

"I'm fine," she answered absently.

"Your father wants to see you immediately. He's been asking for you since—"

"Fine. Thank you, Barbara." Jessica turned and wandered toward her father's office.

Moments later she was sinking into a chair across from her father. "You wanted to see me, Bill?"

"Yes, I—" He looked up at her in shocked surprise. "What happened to you?"

Suddenly aware of how she must look, Jessica simultaneously glanced down at herself and touched her disheveled hair. For one brief second she was horrified, then shrugged and met his eyes. "Nothing."

Bill Mann's eyebrows rose ominously. "Well, where have you been?"

"The beach," she answered evenly.

"Jessica, I'm worried about you. You haven't been yourself lately."

"I'm fine." She folded her hands in her lap. "Now, what can I do for you?"

"Don't try to change the subject. I think you need a vacation. Take a couple of weeks off, you'll feel better after—back on track, so to speak—ready to resume your life."

"I certainly don't have time for a vacation," Jessica said, straightening her shoulders. "With my increased work load, I—"

Bill Mann gestured dismissively. "Don't worry about that. Your schedule will loosen up soon."

Jessica frowned. "That doesn't make any sense. This is our busiest season, not to mention a half dozen new clients—"

He held up his hands. "That isn't why I called you in. We can discuss your taking time off later. Right now I want to discuss the cookie account. Clay's given me his pre-departure report—"

Jessica lifted her head in surprise. "What?"

"Before Clay leaves he always gives me what I call a 'pre-departure report.' Anyway, I wanted your assurance—"

The blood drained from Jessica's cheeks. When she spoke, her voice was thick. "Clay's leaving?"

"He always does," Bill replied mildly. "Surely you're not surprised."

"Yes…no…I mean…" Jessica twisted her hands in her lap, groping for equilibrium. "Leaving?" she repeated in a hoarse whisper.

"Jessica…" Uncomfortable, Bill cleared his throat. "I know what's going on; that is, I know what's been wrong with you, why you've been behaving so out of character."

Jessica raised her eyes and stared blankly at her father. "Excuse me?"

"I know about you and Clay."

Pain was replaced with shock. "But how?"

"Jessica, did you really think you could hide the affair from me? Your own father?"

Heat crept into her cheeks. She felt as if he'd violated her privacy, as if she'd been made a fool of. "Why didn't you say something?"

"I didn't see the need."

Jessica was out of her seat in a flash. She faced him angrily. "You didn't see the need? Instead, you make judgments behind my back—"

"I knew you'd react this way," Bill interrupted wearily. "Besides, what good would a speech from me have done? Could I have talked some sense into you? I think not."

Jessica's eyes narrowed. "What do you mean, 'talk some sense into me'? Spit it out, Father."

"Very well, Jessica." He paused to light a cigarette. "I know how these creative types are." His voice softened. "They're not for you and me, Jessica. They'll never understand what's important to us, what motivates us. I thought you knew that."

The anger of a moment before vanished, being replaced first by disbelief, then distaste. "Us? Them? You sound so elitist."

He patted her hand. "I don't mean to be, Jessica. But in this world there are those who are centered and those who are not. You and I are alike in the fact that we have a goal, a purpose."

"And it's all-consuming, isn't it?"

"It has to be, Jessica. That's the only way to make it to the top."

"Career first," she murmured. "Everything and everyone else take back seats."

"I know it's not always easy. You and Clay were not meant to be, Jessica. In my own way I tried to help you see that."

Her eyebrows drew together. "What do you mean?"

"Never mind, Jessica." He spoke slowly and evenly, as if to a petulant child. "You needn't concern yourself over—"

"I want to know what you meant! Now."

Bill reached across the desk and patted her hand. "I knew from the beginning, as you should have, that this relationship was all wrong for you. I knew that Clay, like your mother, would resent the time you spent on your career. So I—"

"My God!" Jessica interrupted, turning shocked eyes on her father. "Clay was right. All that work you piled on my desk was—" She lifted trembling fingers to her lips. "But it wasn't an endurance test, as Clay suggested. No, you were waiting for me to crack because you knew I'd choose work over Clay. And all along I thought you were trusting me, believing in my ability, but all you wanted was to see me break." She drew a long, steadying breath. "How could you, Father? How could you manipulate me that way?"

"I did it because I love you, Jessica. You have to believe that."

"The way you loved Mother?"

"Yes." Bill Mann stood and faced her. "I loved her. I couldn't believe it when she left. I took good care of her, she wanted for nothing—"

"Except your time," Jessica interrupted. "Except for a little warmth, a little understanding."

He drew his eyebrows together sternly. "Jessica, your mother refused to see what was best for her. I tried, time and again, to channel her energies—"

"That's sick." Her eyes mirrored the disgust in her voice. "I've worked so hard to please you. I've given up everything to prove to you that I'm worthy of your respect. Now I find out you're not worthy of mine."

He blanched at her words; his voice held a trace of desperation. "Jessica, you're so close to being one of the great names in advertising! Just a few more years and you'll have it all. Don't throw away your chance at the top.''

Jessica had waited all her life to hear those words, yet now they brought her no pleasure, no thrill of satisfaction. Instead, an aching emptiness settled over her. She met his eyes. "All? And what will that encompass, Father?"

"Why, you'll have everything I have, everything you've worked for—professional respect, money and power."

"I'm not certain that's enough," Jessica murmured, looking away. After a moment her eyes returned to his. Her voice faltered at first, gaining strength as she spoke. "No...no...it's not. It's not enough."

"Jessica, you really aren't well." In an uncharacteristic gesture, he ran a hand through his hair. "Maybe I should call a doctor—"

"No."

"Some rest...a vacation..."

"No," Jessica repeated vehemently, shaking her head. A smile tilted the corners of her mouth. "I feel better than I have in years." The hint of a smile led to a throaty laugh. "In fact, I feel great!" She checked her watch. "It's after five, Bill. We can continue this discussion, or discuss my future with The Mann Agency during work hours, Monday." She slung her jacket over her shoulder, then crossed to the door. Once there, she looked back at her father's confused face. "Have a good weekend, Bill. I'll see you Monday morning."

Jessica stopped pacing and glanced at the painting hanging above the bed. It was the one Clay had given her; her chest tightened as she looked at it. Where was he? She picked up the phone and dialed Clay's number for what seemed like the hundredth time since leaving her father's office that afternoon. And, like all the others, there was no answer. Where was he? she repeated, slamming down the phone in frustration.

Surely he hadn't left. Surely he hadn't. Jessica resumed her pacing, dragging both hands through her wild hair as she did. She was such a fool. Why hadn't she asked her father when Clay was leaving? She didn't even know when their conversation had taken place.

When was the last time she'd seen Clay? Jessica cocked her head. Two days ago! He could already have left for God knows where, and she would never see him again!

The thought brought a pain so strong and sharp that Jessica sucked in a quick, surprised breath. It couldn't be true, it just couldn't. He wouldn't leave without saying goodbye. She *had* to believe that.

She picked up the phone and dialed again. This time the line was busy. And the next and next. Jessica swore loudly and with gusto. This was ridiculous. Why was she wasting time here, when she could be trying to find Clay? Without pausing for deliberation, she grabbed her car keys and raincoat, then headed out the door.

The drive took twice as long as it should have because of the rain. But it seemed even longer; the whole time she agonized over what Clay's reaction to her declaration would be. By the time she pulled into Clay's driveway, her stomach was in knots and a headache throbbed behind her eyes.

Jessica squinted to see past the rain. His beach house was dark. Would he reject her? Would he laugh in her face and tell her she was too late? She tightened her fingers on the wheel, and considered backing out the driveway and heading straight for Los Angeles.

Hand on the key, she lifted her chin—Jessica Mann didn't run, she told herself firmly. Yanking it from the ignition, she tossed it into her purse. A moment later she was dashing for the house.

There was a tiny overhang above the door, but it didn't help, she was already drenched. Jumping nervously at a violent crack of thunder, she pounded on the door. No answer. She peered inside, unable to see anything, and pounded again. Still no answer.

Her teeth were chattering and she caught her lower lip between them. What should she do now? He could have left in the time it had taken her to drive to Laguna. On the other hand, he might not be able to hear her over the storm.

Inspiration struck and she darted back into the rain, running to the garage window. Standing on tiptoe, she peeked inside, then expelled a long, relieved breath; his motorcycle was parked inside.

Now what? she wondered, water trickling between her shoulder blades and breasts. She could go and find a phone... She shook her head. His phone might be off the hook. She could pound some more or wait on the porch until the rain cleared. Or she could try the windows. A smile tilted her lips—the sliding glass doors and deck. Of course!

Something hit his cheek. It was cold and wet and subtly stinging. Instantly awake, Clay held his breath, adrenaline pumping through him as he realized he wasn't alone. A shadow crossed his line of vision, and he knew without opening his eyes that it was Jessica.

The scent of the rain clung to her, mixing with her own hauntingly familiar perfume; he recognized her breathing. Clay opened his eyes.

She was dripping wet, and her teeth were chattering. His gaze raced over her. She hovered above him, eyes averted, arms crossed in front of her chest. The only light was that of the storm, brilliant but brief behind her, and Clay was struck by the beauty of her profile as it caught the light.

"Jess?"

Her eyes flew to his face, lingered there, then slid away. "I wanted to see you before...Father told me you were..." Her voice quavered, and she took a deep breath. "Father told me you were leaving, and I couldn't let you go without talking to you."

When Clay didn't respond, she crossed to the window. She placed a palm against the cold glass, connecting to the physical world, letting it remind her that this was her last chance at happiness. "This isn't easy for me, Clay." Her laugh was mocking; she swung around. "I was so smug, thought I was so smart. Instead, I was wrong about everything."

She stared at him for a moment, then lowered her eyes. "I met with Mother today and...learned a lot of truths. I met with Father and got a good look at...myself." She wrung her hands. "Clay, I just wanted you to know that...I just wanted to tell you..." Feeling helpless and inadequate, Jessica stared at the floor, hands clasped against her middle, heart beating wildly in her chest.

"What, Jessica?" Clay prompted, his voice raspy.

Her eyes flew to the bed; she cursed being unable to see his expression. "I wanted you to know that you were right...about what I needed, and where I was heading."

"Is that all?"

Blood rushed into her cheeks at the question, and she looked away. "No, I wanted to..." Mustering all her courage, she lifted her chin. "Don't go, Clay. Or, if you must, take me with you."

He expelled a long breath. "Oh, Jess."

Panic fluttered through her. Why didn't he say something? She crossed to the bed and knelt beside it. Gathering his hand into hers, she held it against her damp cheek. "Today Father said the words I'd waited for, gave me the approval I'd worked for. But instead of joy, I felt pain...because you were leaving."

She pressed her lips into the palm of his hand. "I love you, Clay. Take me with you. Please, I don't care where you're going, I just want to be with you."

Clay gently pulled his hand from hers. "No, Jessica. I can't do that."

She released a long, shuddering breath. The sound was filled with despair. Her head drooped; she was too late, she'd lost him.

"Look at me, princess." He tipped up her chin with his index finger. "It wouldn't work. Your career is a part of who you are, a big part. I'd never ask you to give it up. Besides, you can't just give up something you've worked so hard for. You'd never forgive yourself and would end up hating me—"

"No!" She clutched the blanket tightly. "I don't care about success, because it's nothing without you to share it with. Didn't you hear anything I said, Clay? I love you." Suddenly shy, she pressed her face into his shoulder. "I want children, Clay. Our children. I want to go to bed with you every night, wake up with you beside me every morning. I want your smile and our shared laughter. I want to be soft and romantic and vulnerable. Give me a chance, Clay." She lifted tear-filled eyes. "Take me with you!"

"No." He placed a gentle finger against her lips. "I can't take you because I'm not leaving." Clay smiled as her eyes widened. "I can't say I never intended to, because for one brief, insane moment when I went to your father, I thought I could." He pulled her to the bed. "But instead, I realized I was trying to force you into making a decision, the right decision, about us."

"Not leaving? But I thought you loved to travel. I thought—" Confused, her eyes searched his face. "You're staying?"

Clay laughed at the seriousness of her expression and hugged her. "Yes, princess, I'm staying. Now I have a rea-

son to." He gazed at her tenderly. "I love you, Jess. I've
loved you for a long time...maybe since I first saw you
standing in a patch of sunlight, looking so cool and serious."

With his words, muscles tight with stress loosened, the
breathlessness of fear disappeared. Freedom and joy un-
furled inside her like a sail in a sweet, steady breeze. "I love
you, too," she whispered.

Their lips met, parted, clung. For Jessica it was more than
a kiss—it was a promise to love and to cherish, a promise of
forever. And she knew without words that Clay felt the
same. Slowly they undressed, tossing aside sodden garments, laughing at damp bedclothes, sharing an intimacy
that was only possible with commitment.

The lightest brush of his fingertips was heaven, the words
he murmured against her flesh brought a pleasure beyond
language. Jessica sighed and whispered her love as he entered her, her heart near bursting with happiness. And with
the joining of their bodies, she found their mingled excla-
mations and soft sighs a music to rival the classics.

Jessica clung to him as her heart slowed, her flesh cooled.
How could she have been so lucky? she wondered, her eyes
lifting to his. *Not many people get a chance to have it all.*
She pressed her lips against his neck; he smelled of the rain
and their passion. "Now I know what afterglow means,"
she whispered, snuggling closer.

Laughter rumbled in his chest. "I knew you'd come to
your senses and admit you love me."

"And what about you?" Jessica lifted her eyebrows
haughtily. "I wasn't the one leaving town."

Clay laughed and rolled over so she was on top of him.
"Yeah, but I never said I was perfect."

"Mmm," Jessica murmured, nipping his shoulder. His
skin was salty, and liking its sting, she nipped again. She felt

his shudder and smiled. "I can't believe I was so narrow-minded that I refused to see how happy you made me."

"And pigheaded—" he nibbled a tender spot in the curve of her throat "—and stubborn."

Jessica laughed and tangled her fingers in his hair. "You'd better stop now or I'll be forced to find another way to shut you up. And I doubt you have the energy."

He lowered his eyes to her mouth and his voice deepened. "I wouldn't bet money on that." When Jessica's lips parted in silent invitation, he captured them once more. The kiss was slow and thorough. When he pulled away she was breathless. "Jess?"

"Hmm?" Her lids fluttered up.

"I was wondering.... How did you get in here tonight?"

"Oh." A delicate pink tinted her cheeks. "Well, I tried calling—"

"The phone was off the hook."

Jessica sniffed. "Exactly what I thought. So I decided to drive over—"

"Impatient little vixen." Clay grinned as the pink turned to red.

"I pounded on the door, but you didn't hear me above the storm. Anyway, I—" she cleared her throat "—I broke in."

"You what?"

"I tried the windows, but they were all locked. So I . . . well, you know the window above the kitchen sink that faces the deck? Anyway there might be a puddle—"

"Jessica!" Clay fell back against the pillow, roaring with laughter. "I don't believe you did that!"

Jessica bit back a smile. "I don't think it's a good idea to leave those grilling utensils outside. Especially the tongs. They make nifty window smashers and—"

"What," Clay demanded, trying to swallow his laughter but only being partially successful, "has happened to my regal and oh-so-proper Jessica?"

"Well..." Jessica murmured, fluttering her lashes and walking her fingers provocatively up his chest, "a princess can't remain completely unaffected by a barbarian."

"Mmm, I like that." Clay's lips whispered across her cheek. "Jess?"

"Hmm?"

"Remember your earlier comment about energy?"

"Specifically, your lack of?" Jessica's grin was saucy, and she wiggled against him.

"That very one." Clay slipped his hands down to cup her derriere. "I feel my honor is at stake here and would like the opportunity to prove you wrong."

"Prove away," Jessica murmured, bringing her lips to his. "Prove away."

* * * * *

A Trilogy by Diana Palmer

Bestselling Diana Palmer has rustled up three rugged heroes in a trilogy sure to lasso your heart! The titles of the books are your introduction to these unforgettable men:

CALHOUN

In June, you met Calhoun Ballenger. He wanted to protect Abby Clark from the world, but could he protect her from himself?

JUSTIN

Calhoun's brother, Justin—the strong, silent type—had a second chance with the woman of his dreams, Shelby Jacobs, in August.

TYLER

October's long, tall Texan is Shelby's virile brother, Tyler, who teaches shy Nell Regan to trust her instincts—especially when they lead her into his arms!

Don't miss TYLER, the last of three gripping stories from Silhouette Romance!

CHILDREN OF DESTINY

A trilogy by Ann Major

Three power-packed tales of irresistible passion
and undeniable fate created by Ann Major to
wrap your heart in a legacy of love.

PASSION'S CHILD — September

Years ago, Nick Browning nearly destroyed
Amy's life, but now that the child of his
passion—the child of her heart—was in danger,
Nick was the only one she could trust....

DESTINY'S CHILD — October

Cattle baron Jeb Jackson thought he owned
everything and everyone on his ranch, but fiery
Megan MacKay's destiny was to prove him wrong!

NIGHT CHILD — November

When little Julia Jackson was kidnapped, young
Kirk MacKay blamed himself. Twenty years later,
he found her...and discovered that love could
shine through even the darkest of nights.

Don't miss PASSION'S CHILD, DESTINY'S
CHILD and NIGHT CHILD, three thrilling
Silhouette Desires designed to heat up chilly
autumn nights!

SD-445

 # Silhouette Desire

COMING
NEXT MONTH

#445 PASSION'S CHILD—Ann Major
Book One of the CHILDREN OF DESTINY trilogy!
Amy Holland and Nick Browning's marriage of convenience could
turn to passion—if the secret of their child was not revealed....

#446 ISLAND HEAT—Suzanne Forster
When Justin Dunne's search led him to a "haunted castle" and
beautiful Lauren Cambridge, he knew it wasn't the right time to get
involved, unless he could mix business *and* pleasure.

#447 RAZZMATAZZ—Patricia Burroughs
Being stranded in the Reno airport left Kennie Sue Ledbetter with
limited options. Alexander Carruthers came to her rescue, and
somehow the next morning she found herself married...to him!

#448 TRUE COLORS— Mary Blayney
It would take all of television heartthrob Tom Wineski's considerable
charm to convince small-town single mother Janelle Harper he'd
developed a forever kind of passion.

#449 A TASTE OF HONEY—Jane Gentry
Susannah Reid was content with her life...until notorious Jefferson
Cody hit town. He convinced her to start thinking about her own
happiness—not what the neighbors would say.

#450 ROUGHNECK—Doreen Owens Malek
Beau/Landry was a direct contrast to refined lawyer Morgan Taylor.
Beau had done the wrong thing for the right reason, but when he
proposed, would Morgan approve of his tactics?

AVAILABLE NOW:

#439 THE CASTLE KEEP
Jennifer Greene

#440 OUT OF THE COLD
Robin Elliott

#441 RELUCTANT PARTNERS
Judith McWilliams

#442 HEAVEN SENT
Erica Spindler

#443 A FRIEND IN NEED
Cathie Linz

#444 REACH FOR THE MOON
Joyce Thies